Adventures in the Liaden Universe® Number 30

The Gate the Locks the Tree

A Minor Melant'i Play for Snow Season

Sharon Lee and Steve Miller

COPYRIGHT PAGE

The Gate that Locks the Tree: Adventures in the Liaden Universe® Number 30

Pinbeam Books: www.pinbeambooks.com

#

This is a work of fiction. All the characters and events portrayed in this novel are fiction or are used fictitiously.

#

#

THE GATE THAT LOCKS THE TREE is original to this chapbook.

#

Cover design by RL Slather

ISBN: 978-1-948465-07-6 ebook
ISBN: 978-1-948465-08-3 paper

THANK YOU

. . .to Fearless Tyop Hunters and Proofreaders
Kaelin Cordis
Michele Ray
Kate Reynolds
Gala Wind

DRAMATIS PERSONAE

Being the list of players

Vertu Dysan, a taxi driver
Cheever McFarland, Boss Conrad's right hand man
The Tree, a multiple exile
Tommy, a taxi driver
Jemmie, a co-owner
Vertu dea'San, former Delm of Wylan
Yulie Shaper, a farmer
Mary, his spouse
Anna, a kid
Rascal, her dog
Toragin del'Pemridj, a woman who believes in promises
blue-and-red driver, a cabbie who has run through his luck
Chelada, a mother
Talizea, a friend of cats
Miri, her mother
Val Con, her father
Jeeves, a butler
Boss Gotta, a metaphor
Nelirikk, a soldier
Jarome, a cabbie revealed

THE GATE THAT LOCKS THE TREE

A Minor Melant'i Play for Snow Season

ACT ONE

Scene One

In the house of the taxi driver
Enter Vertu and Cheever

Vertu Dysan rose with her lover, both too aware of the coming day's necessities.

Schedules for the week upcoming did not favor long morning comfort, and the wan blueish light of the port was still brighter than the meek dawning of the day-star. An extra hug at the door then, through his bulky coat.

"I'll bring dinner," Cheever said. "No sense going out in the snow."

"More snow?" Vertu said, stepping back and looking up at him.

He grinned.

"Weatherman says there's a squall-line moving in." He shrugged his big shoulders. "Hey, it's Surebleak *and* it's winter. Snow's on the menu."

"I will have something warmer than snow for my late meal, please."

"I'll see what I can do. You drive careful, 'k?"

It was what he said at every parting – *drive careful* – as if she, the taxi driver, was the one who walked in peril.

Still, it warmed her, her Terran lover's tenderness for her, and she smiled, reaching high on her toes to touch his cheek.

"I will be careful. You be careful, also."

"Where's the fun in that?" – again, the usual answer, the half-grin, the serious eyes.

And then he was gone, the door opening and closing so quickly barely a wisp of cold air snuck into the little hallway.

Vertu glanced out the side window, to see him, striding away toward the port. Cheever McFarland, Boss Conrad's Right Hand, had a breakfast meeting waiting on him at the Emerald Casino.

She turned away from the window. Her ride was due in half-an-hour. Time enough to drink her coffee – a taste acquired from Cheever, like she had acquired Surebleak's particular vernacular from Jemmie, and the daily round of her fares.

Cup in hand, she crossed the planned front room library, a challenge still unfilled. The house would grow in time, that she knew, and soon she would unshutter the windows, let light in, and add bookcases and storage – if this was to be her home, she would make it so.

Up the stairs she went, to the bedroom, and pulled on her warmest sweater, with its snow-shedding properties, and walked to the window, sipping from her cup.

She would eat breakfast at Flourpower slightly later, and as the day brightened she saw that Korval's Tree stood a little short against the still perceptible stars … perhaps they would catch that predicted-but-not-yet-arrived squall line, after all.

The bedroom was on the third level of a skinny building in the Hearstrings turf – *her* house, where she had rented a room during her first days of exile, and which she had only recently purchased. The window gave a clear view of the Port Road, and the hill it climbed out of the city. Vertu sipped her coffee and wondered if she was the only one in the city who told the mood of the world by the color the giant at the crest of that long hill showed to first light, and the height. It was more than just height, though – some days the Tree looked fuller, bushier, more open.

Maybe bad weather weighed on the branches. Maybe the Tree purposefully shielded those under it, showing more leaf or less, leaf-top or leaf-bottom as required. Perhaps she should ask Cheever some mythical morning when neither of them was pressed for time.

The upstairs echoed a little now as she hurried toward and down the stairs, for the view of the Tree had nearly hypnotized her, as it sometimes did, as if the Tree felt her gaze and returned it. And why should the Tree not recognize her, as she it? In her fancy, it did, two exiles, making their ways on a strange new world. Why should they not acknowledge each other? For her side, she'd known it the whole of her life, first on Liad where she'd grown up and become Vertu dea'San, Delm of Clan Wylan, or Wylan Herself.

The name on the contract for the purchase of the house, *that* was Vertu Dysan.

She did not bow to Liad anymore; the Tree and its people were here, and she had long since decided that if any one of Clan Wylan wished to speak to her, they could come here, to Surebleak, and meet with Surebleak Port's new Business of the Year co-owner.

It was a quiet house she had, certainly not a rival to Clan Wylan – she'd considered and rejected the local *advertise for a roommate* habit as not being her choice. The house *could* use more company at times – again, there was an echo when she hit the bottom of the stairs in her traction boots – but even with Cheever's potential agreement she doubted she was ready yet to add a child to this place, hollow as it could sometimes be.

Sealing the coat as she hit the entry hall, she glanced to the vidscreen, unsurprised to find the local walks devoid of pedestrians; only a glimmer of vehicle lights, and a blue glow coming down a side street.

Vertu paused, checking her coat seals, glaring into the sky, and its promise of messy driving. There was noise behind the clouds – a rumble she thought wasn't thunder but the latest passenger arrival that meant her afternoon was likely to be busy, snow or rain.

She closed the door behind her as Tommy turned the corner, prompt as always on the one wake-the-day shift he covered every ten days. It was good to have commonplace comforts, and she smiled as he vacated the driver's seat, bowing her in.

Scene Two

In Vertu's taxicab
Enter Yulie, Mary, Anna, Rascal

Vertu's morning shift had been busy, what with the increased mercenary traffic onworld, and much of it carried about town in their cabs – Jemmie's having Tommy Lee as just one of their merc connections, and Vertu herself another – they would need more cars and drivers soon if the merc presence was going to continue increasing. Jemmie had taken to leasing such spare local vehicles as there were, at day-rate, but it hadn't taken long for a half-dozen more cab services to start up, most of them not much more than a car that sort of moved and an idea that there was money to be made.

Twice before lunch, Vertu had seen fare jumpers at work; that, with the weather, infusing the day with more tension than necessary. At times like these, it was good to see the Tree waving in a breeze, but not much chance of that today. She reported the fare jumps to Jemmie's office via com-link when it worked, but the low-power system the Scouts had introduced them to was still highly variable – possibly because it was built with "borrowed" end-of-life equipment, possibly because of Surebleak's own odd planetary make-up.

The problem with Surebleak, she thought, was that it lacked taxi guilds, and even traffic laws. The result was unsafe cars, and incompetent drivers, with no sense of … Balance. Denying so Liaden a concept still left the problem of drivers like the ones who drove the garishly red and blue striped cars – she thought there were two of them, both usually hatless, a stupidity in a Surebleak winter. One of them had several times in the last few days followed her, and tried to arrive before she did at groups standing near the road. A guild, an association, a club – *something* would need to be done. She shook her head, Terran-style then – perhaps she should bring it to one of the Road Bosses. Well … maybe she should talk to Jemmie first.

Vertu's breakfast at Flourpower was a distant memory and the carry-away grab-lunch was hours gone by the time she stopped at Reski's to drop off a pair of fares and take on more coffee. The house specialty was a decent bean-based scrapple handwich if she had time to order one! – and not being waved down immediately for another ride, she took an actual break, calling in as off-duty despite the com unit's buzz, side-parking the cab a half-block away, and stretching her legs while she leaned into the sudden fine snowmizzle that seemed incongruous coming from clouds *that* dark.

Well, they promised *some*thing, those clouds, and, as warm as it was at the moment, the mizzle might actually turn to rain. Her fares had all been concerned about the weather, since it had been cold enough lately that rain might slick into ice on the slightest excuse. On Liad, of course, rain had always meant an uptick in her business, but here? Here she was too straight out to have rain be anything more than a bother. Ice would be another matter entire.

The precipitation hid the Tree on the hill from sight; even so, she *felt* its location, just like she had when she'd been driving her taxi in Solcintra, port and city. The Tree was a magnet; part of her landscape, visible or hidden.

Reski's was packed with hungry people, but she got noticed quick and probably ahead of others – with a *Jemmie's Taxi* hat on her head she was recognized as much as a public service as a business – and she was glad not to be trying to pack herself into the grid of crowded tables.

The cab had more room than one of Reski's tables, so long as she didn't fill it with passengers.

She was back to the taxi in less than a half hour, carrying two full coffee cups and a triple handwich pack. There were two people waiting near the cab, tucked into the slight protection of a leather shop's overhanging sill, a number of bags at their feet. There was a dog nearby, too, and a youth. Vertu sighed. This was one of the more difficult parts of her job, sorting out who got to go first and who had to be left behind.

She hurried past, opened the cab, and showed the *On Break* card. One of those in the doorway – wearing an orange cap – nodded, and leaned in closer under the overhang.

Vertu sealed the door, and grabbed half a handwich. She played music over the speaker while she ate, and drank some coffee.

She closed her eyes, and counted to twelve twelve times. Opening her eyes, she turned the *On Break* card face down on the dashboard, brushing crumbs to the road as she opened.

The kid and the dog circled in from their explorations down the walk while the two in the doorway stepped out, each grabbing a couple of bags. The one in the orange hat, Vertu saw, was Yulie Shaper, and his coat looked like it might be new. She'd seen him not long ago, having gone as Cheever's guest to Lady yo'Lanna's arrival reception, and he'd been wearing what looked like new there, too. Good on him, as they said here, things must be picking up!

"Where do we go?" Vertu asked. "Who arrived first?"

Yulie laughed, and it was a good laugh for someone with a reputation of being distant if not entirely elsewhere most of the time.

"All got here at once, that's how it is, since we come down together we're all going to the same place."

Now Vertu recognized the dog and the kid – Anna, that was the kid, connected to Boss Nova's place – she didn't remember the dog's name but the kid was hardly around without it, and the woman with them someone else she'd seen around, always walking at her own pace and not usually a cab user that Vertu knew of. Yes. She had been at the reception, too; and the source of some merriment, too. Her name, Vertu thought, was Mary – another one of the folks who had been living quietly come suddenly to light. Odd that it took an influx of strangers from outworld to make the locals stand forward.

"All together, then," she said with what she hoped was an encompassing nod.

"Load up."

This they did with swift efficiency. Vertu, seeing all in hand, slid into her seat, and keyed the heater for more warm air.

"Where do we go?" she asked again, unlocking the doors all around.

The girl jumped into the front seat, calling out.

"Rascal, here!"

But the dog had run ahead of the cab, ears perked, sniffing, looking – up.

"Haysum!"

That was Yulie, looking in the same direction as Rascal, where barely a block away the world looked like it was being closed behind a sudden curtain of heavy snow. The snow engulfed them with an audible susurration, the flakes as big as tea saucers.

The adults got into the back seat, tucking themselves around the bags, wiping snow from faces and gloves.

"Rascal!"

The dog turned and jumped through the door into the girl's lap. The door sealed, and the girl cuddled the dog – whether for the dog or herself was difficult to tell, Vertu thought, upping the heat again.

"We're going to my place – our place," said Yulie Shaper. "All the way up Undertree Hill – Port Road's your best route, in this. Just go left right before you get to the gate that locks the Tree in...."

Vertu tapped on the steering wheel for several moments, considering the route, and reflecting on the phrase, "the gate that locks the Tree…" before she put the cab into driving mode.

"Do you think," she said, as she waited for a truck to pass them slowly before she pulled out into traffic, "that the Tree minds being locked in? What of the Road Bosses? I never thought about it like that before."

Beside her Anna pursed her lips in consideration, and from the back a couple of noncommittal hems and haws happened.

Yulie finally ventured a word….

"It was me said it, and I never really thought about it that way, either, truthtelled. It's not like the Bosses or the Tree is *really* locked in, at least not for long; I figure they're all where they wanna be, don't you? I mean, I like where I growed up and I'm still there, and that's kind of what they have, isn't it, give or take a thousand light years or so. But the Bosses and the Tree, they got things they hafta do to keep the world right …."

Yulie let his pensive consideration stall while Vertu avoided one of the striped taxis that was barely making headway in the opposite direction. The windscreen on that one was showing an ice build-up already, making Vertu pleased that she and Jemmie agreed on maintenance rules and schedules. Difficult to drive when the windscreen was full of snow.

They drove in silence, Rascal's tail ticking a happy rhythm on Anna's coat sleeve, accepting the belly scritches the girl lavished while peering through their own spotless windscreen, the cones of on-coming lights and the sudden looming of passing cars bringing ears to alert.

"A traveler, your dog," Vertu offered, "likes to be on point!"

Anna nodded, scritched the top of the dog's muzzle teasingly.

"Also, lazy a little, maybe. Rascal does not often get to travel this way, and being in front is a treat for both of us – right, Rascal?"

For her trouble Anna got her chin licked and some dog-breathy ear sniffs as Vertu slowed the vehicle to a walking pace behind several wind-whipped pedestrians leaning into the snow as they crossed the street at an oblique angle.

Snow muffled the wind just as it muffled the road noise, a gritty squealing vibration permeating the car as Vertu ducked their path close to the sidewalk and behind the walkers. The windshield's airjets weren't sufficient to the task now so she activated the wipers in the gloom. Dusk was still over an hour away but this – this would take concentration.

"Hush, Rascal," Anna said then, low and serious. "We all need to listen and watch in case there's a problem going up the hill. Watch hard. Might be a problem on the hill. You too, Mary, watch hard!"

A flutter of concern tightened Vertu's gut now, an edge of nerves down the back of her neck, a touch of extra speed to her eye motions. She didn't often feel these things, but she had learned to pay attention to them, despite that her delm had put her youthful mention of such tensions aside with a terse, *you're no Healer, girl.*

"Quiet," the girl whispered, and her head moved… ah, looking for the driver-info on the dashboard….

"Oh, no, – Miss Vertu – not you, you're watching good already. And Yulie sees a lot more than anyone knows, 'cept maybe Mary. But we should *all* pay attention, in weather like this."

"Anna?"

That was Mary, and clearly the question had levels within levels.

Anna glanced over her shoulder, shrugged, made a quick hand-motion, said a word that slid past Vertu's ears, and continued.

"Probably nothing for us. For us we have Miss Vertu, who is a very good driver. But this snow, it – the situation is unsettled."

The girl had the right of it; the situation was unsettled. Vertu got them to the outskirts at Port Edge and then into the jumble of traffic at Grady's Crossroads, a jumble made harder to sort by the number of pedestrians and their uniform unwillingness to give way before anything on wheels. They waited at one point for five minutes until Yulie had her pull over while he and Mary enlisted as volunteers, joining half a dozen others. They finally managed to untangle a three car confusion where one car had gotten wedged between two others.

Vertu restarted the clock when her passengers returned to her, brushing snow off each other, and laughing.

At last, they were through the intersection and on the Port Road itself, headed out of town, and up the hill.

Scene Three

In Vertu's taxicab, on the Port Road. Outside, a blizzard.

Progress was slow; Jemmie called on the radio to make sure the car was in motion, at least, and Vertu's confirmation of a fare in progress to a known destination was welcome.

"You call in when you get to the top, hear me? We got folks wanting a ride, but I'm thinking we're all best just staying put. This is a wallop of a storm all of a sudden; couple the old-timers say we'll be lucky to move anything much on the road tomorrow, much less tonight. So you *call me*, Vertu, before you head back down. Promise."

"I promise," Vertu said mildly, as if Jemmie wasn't younger than her youngest daughter.

"That's all right, then. You drive careful."

Vertu had already driven through a Surebleak winter, and seen two storms that the locals had grudgingly awarded the accolade *bad 'un.* This storm though, this was, in Vertu's opinion, shaping up to be something other than a mere *bad 'un.* This one was *a worrier.*

She got them through a small intersection where two cars had been pushed to the side, quiescent. Periodically the vibration transmitted from the road to the taxi changed … oddly.

"Graupel," said Yulie, "in layers with some sleet and then with fling-snow. Slick as – " and here he paused, considering, perhaps, the ears of the girl, before continuing, "slick like skin ice from a rain it can be. We're good though, our Miss Vertu's got us on course, all good."

About that, Miss Vertu herself was less confident – and in the next moment realized what exactly was wrong with the light approaching them.

"Wrong side!" Yulie said sharply.

Vertu slowed the cab to a stop while the other vehicle – a small panel truck – continued down what must have been the gravel edge of the wrong side of the road at a breathtakingly slow pace.

"Flo's Grocery Wagon?" Mary read the side of the truck as it passed. "They're city-based. What is it doing up here?"

"Musta been up to Lady yo'Lanna's place!" said Yulie. "Geez, ain't got no sense, city or else, 'noring oncoming traffic!"

By now dusk had edged into dark, with other traffic nonexistent. There were tracks in the road, but the snow and breeze were working together to fill them in, leaving vague ruts. Vertu wondered about the van's driver, seeing several places where it appeared the ruts wandered off the road entirely, but there – parallel ruts – must have been other traffic going one way or another.

Questioned, Vertu would have told anyone that she knew the Port Road well, but in the dark, with the snow blowing it wasn't clear to her exactly where she was, and with two major turns – surely she couldn't have negotiated those without knowing it! – she missed the Tree's presence as a guide and found herself peering into the snow's star field as if --

Hah! Likely that was….

But she heard Anna give an intake of breath and then Yulie, who'd been leaning comfortably against Mary in the back, sat up straighter.

"Yanno," he said, "sometimes we get weather a little different on top the hill than at the bottom; I think we might not have that slick ice under us now – haven't heard that grind! We're not too far away from that turn at Chan's Pond, I'm thinking. See, there's the pointer rock for that slick twisty part – kinda looks different under snow, though, if you don't know it."

Vertu *didn't* know it, and barely made out a lump three times the size of the car lurking just by the right edge of the road. She tried to imagine the thing dry and unshrouded by snow, sunlit on an early fall day and – failed.

The snow and gathered darkness had her driving by instinct now. She recalled that there were more than a few twisty parts to the road, and if she remembered correctly, this part was twistier but not as steep and angled as the next, *very sharp*, turn.

Rascal mumbled a complaint on the seat next to her and Anna shifted him so that his shoulder leaned more against the side window. He peered at – and possibly through – it, vague trails of smoke rising from his nostrils.

Anna spoke then; another word again that Vertu missed hearing. Yulie didn't catch it either, and he said so.

"Anna, not thinking I got that clear ..."

She looked over her shoulder briefly, then at Vertu.

"It was for Rascal. He's got fidgets and I asked him to stay still. I think he's been seeing the wavy tracks off on this side and he's worried."

"Might be. Can't see 'em so good, myself. You watch hard, then. Tell Rascal we're not letting a little snow get in the way of giving him his dinner!"

The girl whispered something to the dog; his fidgets grew quieter.

Vertu shrugged tension out of her shoulders. She'd been unconsciously using those very same tracks as a guide while avoiding them because they affected traction and also because they tended, in her estimation, to hug the edge far too closely.

Briefly, Vertu was sure she knew exactly where they were. The slow motion exaggerated the twists, and she knew this as one of the spots she enjoyed driving a little harder into on dry days, without snow. The acceleration here could be exhilarating, the car willing to grab at the road and allow the driver to fling it this way and that.

She smiled. *That* was the kind of driving she was required to deplore in her underlings, of course – officially, but there, a useful kind of training it was sometimes to know how the car might act at the edge of control.

Vertu allowed the taxi to slow now, the tracks before her an odd jumble.

"He's driving scared," Anna said with the kind of forcefulness that brooked no doubt. See? He ran off the side of the road. The – "

She stopped as if she'd caught herself being a Seer. On Liad, Vertu had twice driven those in the throes of their Sight – and the girl sounded as if she might be on that route.

Hugging Rascal, Anna turned to speak to her.

"Liad does not have such weather?"

Vertu answered, wondering why this question *now*.

"There are parts of Liad that have snow in some seasons, but not so much – and in any wise, no such storms as we have here."

She might have said more, but she was startled into silence, as the scene beyond the windscreen grew momentarily bright as early dawn, the blowing snow drifting across their vision and sharing the light an eerie moment or two before thunder bounced about the cab. Rascal whined, the humans all gasped. The light lessened, came back twice, both times with the shock of nearby thunder, before the storm deepened and there was the sound of hail bouncing off the cab's roof and windshield before their world was again the small tunnel of light they carried with them.

"There's a problem," Anna said abruptly. "She's out of patience. They're all scared and she's ready!"

Rascal whined.

Mary asked, "Who, Anna? Where?"

Anna shrugged, the dog pushing his head against her shoulder.

"Where – ahead of us. I don't know who, but she is ahead of us – up!"

ACT TWO

Scene One

Beset in the belly of the storm

Enter Toragin, the blue-and-red driver, Chelada

"Understanding the theory is not the same as understanding the fact."

The delm had uttered those words to the nadelm. The nadelm had discoursed upon them at length several times afterwards to *his* mother – the delm's sister, who had also been present – and several times more to the rest of the household, including the lesser children of his siblings, of which large group Toragin del'Pemridj was the least, in terms of both age and in the regard of the nadelm.

Toragin had herself been present when those words were uttered and had been permitted a second drink of the morning wine on that occasion, it having been the morning when the sky grew dark, the valley echoed and rumbled, the horizon changed – and, well, *every*thing had changed. Toragin was here, now, on Surebleak because – precisely because – of that morning when Clan Korval, and, more importantly, Clan Korval's Tree – had vanished from Liad.

The theory, back then, was simply that a space vehicle would approach Liad's surface and remove Korval's house. Of the family, perhaps the delm's sister, Toragin's grandmother, had the best idea of what that had *meant*, she having spent ten Standards as an orbital mining engineer before having been ordered home to produce multiple heirs for multiple contract husbands. Her skills running to administration, once home she'd not escaped into space again, nor had she found it easy to reenter society. So, she had spent more time in the company of cats than of people, achieving a certain serenity for herself and her like-minded assistants amidst the bustle and intrigues of an ambitious clan.

Being the closest clan house but one to Korval's Valley had always meant that a peculiar peace informed Lazmeln's clanhouse, for the city was kept at a distance by geography and the agreements made with the first captains. Then, with the changes, those ancient agreements fell. Tourists, spies, and opportunists traveled the local roads – serenity was broken for Clan Lazmeln's in-house overseer as well as for the delm.

Theory now –

But, no. This was *not* theory. This was reality. Toragin was hungry, colder than she'd ever been in her life, and more afraid than she would allow herself to know, much less Chelada.

Chelada the Determined, Toragin thought, but this time, in this reality, she did not smile. Chelada's determination had brought them here.

Chelada's determination might see them die here.

That, too, was reality – or, rather, a possible reality, looming much too close.

And in this reality that was not theory, Toragin considered that as afraid – terrified! – as she had been when Korval's clanhouse and Tree were scooped up from Liad and taken away, this was the first time that her life, and Chelada's, was actually in danger. To have come this far with so little trouble beyond that of convincing Lazmeln Herself that this journey was necessary to honor and to Lazmeln's continued peace – to have come so far, and so quickly, only to meet bleak disaster, lost in the snow within grasp of the goal!

Who could have imagined a world this wild? A world in which anti-collision devices were turned *off* on vehicles during a storm because the snow and ice registered as threat; a world where vehicles might ignore the road entire, or force each other off-route despite lights and flashing markers?

Their driver, Toragin thought, had done well to avoid the collision. Going over the event in her mind she again saw the lights loom out of the snow, saw those lights continuing to aim at them, as if they were a target. She felt the cab slide, grab, and turn away, hands breadths separating them from the small road which was their proper route, and then on. She recalled the driver saying, "Best if we keep momentum here, I think this road comes back into Port Road a little way ahead, and we got good gravel!"

"We are going the wrong way!" she protested. "We are going *away* from the Tree!"

"All roads here gotta aim up that way," the driver countered. "The side roads connect back into the Port Road."

This sounded as if he knew his territory and Toragin was prepared to allow herself to be calmed, until he added, not quite under his breath.

"Pretty sure so, anyhoots."

It was too late by then, and Toragin sat in the front seat, Chelada snug in the back, her conveyance against a heat vent. They both sat, and allowed the driver to do his work, while they felt the presence of the Tree, not ahead of them anymore, but to the right of the cab's slippery route. Too far to the right.

Still, the driver had been doing well in keeping his vehicle on the snow-covered road. As the route began to turn, slowly, back to the right, Toragin had begun to relax in truth, thinking that it could not be so far, now –

Lightning ripped through the grey curtains of snow, startling, disorienting even before the thunder boomed.

The driver started, jerking the wheel in his astonishment. The tires were forced off of the safe gravel onto solid ice.

The taxi spun around, twice; the vaunted momentum giving way to a fading slide.

The slide was slow, nearly silent, ending in a lurch, and a crunch as the road edge turned to leafed-over mud covered by ice.

"Sleet! Crud! Graupel and sludge!"

The driver hit the dashboard with a mittened fist.

Using the shock webbing, Toragin dragged herself more-or-less upright, and stared into the back seat.

"Chelada!"

There came a *huff* from the blanket-covered resting place, and a touch along her inner senses, as if a pink tongue had licked her nose. Toragin relaxed. Chelada was not pleased – well, and who might blame her? – but she had not been hurt.

"Taxis!" the driver was continuing his rant. "Easy money, she says. How tough can it be to drive around all day?"

Toragin took a deep breath, and closed her eyes. She could feel the Tree, up the hill, still too far to the right. How far, she wondered? Could she walk to it from here? More to the point, could she walk to the Tree in the teeth of a lightning-laced snowstorm, with the snow already fallen perhaps to her knees, *and* carrying Chelada?

Well, no, she admitted to herself. Perhaps not.

Definitely not.

The driver had stopped cursing.

"Miss?" he said.

She opened her eyes and looked at him.

"Yes?"

"Will that thing live if you let it go? It has fur; I saw it. Don't know that the car's power packs are going to last long enough for this to stop and us to get found. If we gotta walk out, that's gonna be a long walk, and you don't wanna be carrying extra. Can you –"

Toragin recoiled in horror.

"Abandon Chelada! No!"

The driver sighed, nodded.

"I'm gonna go out and take a look at how we're in, Miss. Might be we can rock 'er out. If we can't get moving, we could all freeze, and in not too long!"

Toragin put a hand out as he turned toward his door.

"Comm?" she said. "Radio? Can we call for help?"

The driver smiled – perhaps it was a smile – and shook his head.

"Nah, no radio on this one. Cheap doin's, right? Who needs a radio?"

"I'm going out now. You watch me, OK? If I go down, I'd take it kindly if you tried to get me back into the cab."

The only light in the car was a vague red glow from the sparse instruments. The driver was pulling his stretch cap far down on his head, covering his ears, while he stared into the windscreen as if were a mirror in truth and not simply covered in snow.

The wind screamed suddenly, and the cab rocked. Toragin held her breath; she thought the driver did, too.

"Right," he said, and looked to her.

"Miss, I want you to use this shovel when I start to push on the door, and try to keep the snow away from the side I got to go through, so it don't fill up the car or freeze the lock. Can you do that?"

"Yes," Toragin said without conviction. She wasn't used to people – other than cats, of course – depending on her strength. Still, it wasn't as if she was weak, after all. She'd been almost strong enough to keep up with *all* the older children around the house, children who pushed and played secret nasty games of shoving, who risked being denounced to a half-distracted tutor because, after all, who would *believe* that the elders – the oh-so-well-behaved elders would torment the clan's precious youngers?

"Pull the hood, Miss, your hood. When I open up you'll want it. Cover that cage up good, too, if that thing needs to be warm."

Toragin bristled.

That thing.

Cage.

It.

On Liad there would have been Balance due … except not really, for on Liad both Toragin and the cats were – among those who knew of them at all – just another of Clan Lazmeln's aberrations.

Chelada was ignoring everything. She was being patient. So *very* patient. She had nothing to say to the driver; he was beneath her notice. Toragin, she trusted to take everything in hand. That was Toragin's function, after all. In the meanwhile, she arranged herself against the heat vent, and slipped into a dream-state. For a moment, Toragin thought wistfully of slipping into sleep, to awake when all inconveniences had been solved.

"OK, here's how we work it," said the driver. "I'm gonna get out, like I said. Gonna clean off the windscreen, and take a walk around the cab, see where's the tires, zackly, and what's the best angle to rock 'er. You keep the snow outta the door and watch me. Right?"

"Right," said Toragin, so faintly she didn't even convince herself.

The shovel arrived to hand and the driver heaved against the door, fighting drifts and wind, until of a sudden, it was open, and he slipped out.

Cold and wind seeped in, and then all heat fled as the crystals of ice flowed around the opening, top and bottom.

Toragin dutifully used the shovel, pushing the snow away from the door, squinting against the blowing snow, the wind howling in her ears, awed by the power of the storm.

There were places on Liad where it snowed, but Liad's weather was well-tracked and one needn't generally be where it might snow unless snow was the goal. Here weather was never so well-behaved. It had said as much in the planetary guide, when she had researched Surebleak, but – understanding the theory is not the same as understanding the fact.

The driver leaned in at the top of the door, holding on with a gloved hand. Between the wind and the uncertain footing the position looked precarious. The driver's voice was strained as he pointed toward the back seat.

"Miss, if you can reach that broom and hand it out?"

Toragin turned, awkwardly seized the implement and dragged it over the seat, turning back in time to hear a muffled yell. She caught a glimpse of a gloved hand tracing a clear spot on the window glass as it slid, and there was another yell, this time of pain, as something thumped on the side of the taxi.

The car door fell back, closing with a dull thud.

Chelada complained.

"Out," she said quite clearly. "Toweeell."

"Oh, not now!" Toragin's voice carried a desperate overtone against the wind and clatter of snow.

"Help me, Miss, I'm under!"

Under? What could that mean?

Under?

What?

Chelada spoke again.

"Towellll!"

#

Towels.

Fiber towels from the roll helped staunch the blood – Toragin had never seen so much blood in her life. The driver's legs were both scraped and bleeding. She thought that was all the trouble, and certainly enough, and dragged the driver out from beneath the vehicle by hauling on one arm, while he used the other in a swimming motion against the snow.

Then, with blood on her gloves and the driver's cold-weather undersuit struggling to keep temperature they'd both tried to rise.

It was obvious instantly, as they'd held onto the door and pulled, that there was some kind of urgent damage to the driver's right leg. Or to the foot.

Toragin was no med-tech, though she had some training in identifying and treating veterinary issues like blocked urinary tracts, pregnancy, hairballs. She didn't *think* she was looking at a broken leg, but even light touches to the side of the leg, low down, and the top of the foot, showed serious swelling. There was bleeding, too, which she wrapped with a precious cleaning cloth meant for Chelada – the leg didn't feel right to her – might there be a splinter of bone *there*?

"Can you drive?" asked the driver, panting. "There's no autopilot in this thing."

"Aren't we stuck?" she countered.

A pause then, while the wind counterpointed the silence of the cab. There were clicks that matched the rhythm of the flashing yellow, green, and red lights outside the cab, and there was Chelada's breathing, getting louder like it did when she was going into a deep sleep.

Finally the driver spoke.

"We are stuck, but maybe not so bad. Might be able to pull it loose, if you can drive it. Else ..."

From the back seat came Chelada's worried mutter. Yes, thought Toragin. First, they had to arrange the inside of the cab so that she could occupy the driver's seat.

The best bet, all things being what they were with that foot, was either for the driver to let Toragin climb over him, possibly dislodging the cab, or –

"I can try to walk around," Toragin said.

"Don't fall, but try. Very slick!"

With snow and wind flapping the hood of her coat she managed to walk around the front of the car, avoiding the slick streaks where the driver's worn boots had lost traction and carried them and their occupant well under the car.

Opening the door was harder – the driver having dragged himself into the other seat there wasn't sufficient purchase for a one-legged push on the door to be much help. Chelada's voice from the back seat gave Toragin an extra urgency – she was afraid she'd heard *that* sound from an expectant cat-mother before.

"Point and shoot," the driver said. "You engage the car with this button and just aim it. Now, my plan was to go really really *really* slow to try to get some traction, and then aim, like I said, along this little ridge. Aim just to the right of the ridge at first, and then when we get purchase, you'll turn it, just a little, back toward the rest of the road. That ought to do it!"

Toragin's experience as a fair-weather driver was hard to translate to this spot, this *now*.

The doing, after a few minutes of effort, just didn't. Tires spun and the car chattered side-wise just the smallest bit, ending up, so Toragin thought, even deeper in the morass of snow and ice. The rest of the road was either across the ice ridge in front of them, if the turn-loop they'd used to avoid the on-coming lorry was traversable at all, or it was behind them by multiple car lengths.

Breathing was loud in the car, again. Toragin could see the driver dabbing at one gashed leg slightly.

"If I take the shovel and dig until I reach dirt, can I put that under the wheels and ..."

The driver considered her briefly.

"Not snowbred, are you? I mean, you just about got me in the car, with us both working. You think you have snow-shifting muscles? Can you move gravel that's froze together? Gets hard fast."

There was more silence. In the back seat, Chelada's breathing was faster and louder.

The driver spoke again.

"How much did your boots cost? Where'd you get 'em? Did someone help you or did you just buy them off the rack?"

Toragin bristled. She doubted she'd ever talked about the cost of anything with a casual stranger and why now?

"That's not something I share!"

"Calm down, Miss. I can't go nowhere with this leg. Cab's stuck. I'm trying to figure if we can get you to walk out for help or not, and if you bought cheap or stupid, it ain't gonna work."

ACT THREE

In the Hall of the Mountain King

Enter Talizea, Miri, Jeeves, Val Con, the Tree, clowders of cats and kindles of kittens

Uphill the wind was stronger than on the roads below, the flattened plateau a left-over of Surebleak's early days, when the company used this spot to prove their claim and take the first modest dense-lode of timonium.

On one side of the road, not quite as exposed to the weather, due to being tucked back into a grove of small sturdy trees, Yulie Shaper's holding huddled against the storm. A goodly-sized property, with house and outbuildings above ground, most of the real holdings were subsurface. Long-dormant market gardens were coming into their own after generations of disuse.

Also above-ground, between house and subterranean gardens, a small, brave Tree, in fact a planted branch of the larger Tree in whose shadow it lay in the evenings of the summer's brighter days – did not so much huddle as dare the winds that shook it.

If the larger Tree communicated with the smaller there was no sign of it amidst the fury of the storm. The large Tree stood shoulders above the rest of the plateau, dwarfing the vehicles parked on the outside of the small fenced drive as well as the several more inside that were not garaged. For that matter the Tree dwarfed the house that circumscribed the Tree's ancient trunk. A walker outside the gates might have noticed the way the Tree absorbed the local winds, might have realized that the spirals and eddies carried snow that had not only been deflected from the house and Tree but from the nearby grounds, and to a lesser extent even the smaller Tree was spared the worst of the storm's abuses.

Outside, then, snow and wind, filling the air with energy.

Inside Jelaza Kazone, the house, the wind was distant, the fallen snow as much as the ancient stone serving to muffle the roar. The directed energies moderated by the Tree's gathering and dropping of snow, by the local wind patterns born under the branches and reaching out to the very edges of the plateau were invisible inside, even to those with surveillance cameras available.

Though it was quieter inside the house than out, the storm's energies still made themselves felt to the inmates.

Talizea was particularly alert to the storm. She, like a number of the other residents, had never experienced a storm quite like this – indeed, the *house itself* had in all of its many Standards never had seen so much snow in such a short time, so much wind burdened with so much precipitation all at once. The child was not quite comfortable with the wind-sounds, muffled as they were, and her edge of alertness gathered around her and drifted onto others.

Talizea's cats – for usually she had an honor guard of two or three – were this evening increased by a half dozen, or perhaps more. The cats shifted position as if taking point when a particular blast of air from the northeast slammed the same windows twice.

The child's mother, Miri, was also alert to the wind. The other sounds she knew from her past, especially the sound of snow sliding, peeling from a wall or window ledge or branch, to fall with a slow whomp. Miri doubted she'd ever felt this safe or this warm in a storm like this as she did tonight, but – she'd never had her child in hand during a blizzard; so she, too, was alert.

The cook and other staff walked carefully, listening. They too, with decades of experience in-house, and generations of back-story, were new to this kind of storm, and this *much* storm. Even Jeeves, butler, security, and possibly the best military mind in the system – wandered the floor as if calculating and cataloging all the new sounds and all the potential dangers. His wheels played the floorboards like a xylophone, the ancient wood toned by the feet of generations of clan members.

It was perhaps the robot's musical movements that brought Val Con yos'Phelium from the delm's office, where he had been called to speak with the so-called boss of Surebleak Transport. Mr. Mulvaney's plan was to consolidate several local small trucking operations under his company's name, and thus gain the benefits of numbers for all. It was a plan ill-suited to Surebleak and the current regulations governing the Port Road. Still, Mr. Mulvaney *kept in touch*, but never during the Road Bosses office hours.

Finishing the call with less than the abruptness it merited, Val Con stepped out of the office, aware of Jeeves' pacing, of the wind, and something … else. At first, it seemed to be Tree-touch; on consideration, though – not entirely so. Was the storm so desperate that it *concerned* the Tree?

Now, *there* was an unsettling thought.

Val Con tarried another moment, trying to remember the last time the Tree had seemed – concerned. Nothing came to mind.

Which was possibly *even more* unsettling.

Frowning slightly, he moved down the hall, silent in soft house shoes, heading for the room that had become Jelaza Kazone's center.

The ruckus room was quiet, where quiet encompassed the snoring of cats, the wrestling of kittens, the crackle of paper as Talizea fingered her book; and another, as Miri turned a page.

They sat together in the pillow corner, tucked comfortably under the same blanket. There were cats atop the blanket, curled next to the quiet readers, several purring.

Val Con dropped to the blanket beside Talizea, rescuing his own book from under the chin of Merekit, who found every object a pillow.

"I am released," he said.

"'bout time," Miri commented, looking up at him with a lopsided grin. "Like to find who gave that *loobelli* the delm's comm number."

"That would be interesting," Val Con agreed. The sound of wheels rolling along wood caught his attention, and he called out.

"Jeeves, will you join us?"

"At once, Master Val Con."

Indeed, almost immediately the door opened silently and the robot's headball flashed blue-and-violet greetings to Talizea, who laughed and, lacking a headball with the appropriate capabilities, flapped her hands in reply.

More cats arrived in the wake of the butler. They, like Val Con, seemed to have ears lifted, trying to track a sound they could not quite hear.

"Jeeves, tell me if you might, is there something amiss? Are we forgetting something, overlooking a small thing that needs done? Have we already forgotten something? Is there a … a problem? Is the house – unsettled?"

Jeeves, who could instantaneously send pinbeams across space, who could directly read the planetary defense nets, who could communicate with intelligences far from human, flashed a subdued fog-green to the assembled.

"I understand the question to be: Is the house unsettled? Working."

Val Con and Miri, Road Boss, Delm of Korval, looked at each other.

"*Working*?" Miri repeated.

"Apparently so."

Val Con glanced about, taking in the sheer numbers of whiskers on display.

"Do we *have* this many cats, *cha'trez*?"

He swept his arm out, encompassing those in the room, and inferring as yet untold numbers in the halls.

One of the newcomers – a fluffy grey cat with large black feet – caught Val Con's eye.

"Is that not Yulie's favorite? Jeeves, have they all come to us for safety in the storm? Is there danger?"

Jeeves repeated the word, head ball flashing. "Danger?"

"Working still?"

Val Con and Miri exchanged another glance, each feeling the other trying to shrug off unease.

At that moment, came the sound of thunder – a distant rattle – then more, like cannon fire near the front gates. Val Con snapped to his feet as cat ears swiveled.

Silence followed, soft *whomps* were more felt than heard, as the thunder-shaken snow fell from the branches of the Tree, visible through the windows overlooking the inner garden.

Talizea looked around, an expression of grim concentration on her small face. Several cats detached themselves from nearby clowders and came over to her, draping themselves across her lap and tucking against her sides.

Jeeves gave what might be termed a *mutter* in a human, a small sound of frustration or disbelief.

"Sir," he said formally, head-ball a steady pale orange. "As usual, you have astutely assessed the situation. The cats – all of them – find the weather to be unusual. The cats from Liad, you understand, are not yet entirely acclimated – they have perhaps not assimilated all the tales and information shared by the local cat clans. The local cat clans are not yet fully synced, you might say, with the information shared by the cats who have lived undertree, and who of course bear the memories of the generations who went before."

"Among the cats, there is uncertainty. The Tree is uncertain as well."

Miri rose and leaned gently against Val Con's side, arms folded tightly across her chest.

"So," she said, "being uncertain makes the cats unsettled, which we feel, since the cats bring us so much news?"

She unfolded her arms – tapped Val Con on the shoulder –

"You been holding out on me, Tough Guy? Tree been slipping you inside information?"

"*Cha'trez*, I think the Tree has not been in touch with me today, certainly not to the point of passing coded messages via the cats!" He paused.

"Jeeves, I wonder if you might be able to tell me exactly how you and the Tree communicate, or you and the cats? How is it that you know that the Tree is unsettled if it has not shared this directly with me?"

The head-ball brightened momentarily.

"I believe that I cannot precisely explain that, sir," Jeeves said earnestly. "It does seem that certain of the – means – of sharing information among us all are less sharply defined than they might be, almost a matter of habit rather than content.

"But on the day, yes, the energy level has been strange in the lower atmosphere. That, combined with an unpredicted bomb cyclone, resulted in the storm growing much larger than expected. That led to a – revelation of error, and – forgetfulness, on the part of the Tree."

Miri put a hand on Val Con' shoulder, then settled her chin on it. With her other hand she made a rolling motion –

"Please go on," she said, "if there's more."

"Yes, thank you. It appears that something has been forgotten, or understood – incorrectly. Now that it has come clear to me, I must inform you that there are visitors on the way."

"Visitors," Miri repeated, and Val Con added.

"On the way from where, I wonder? I mean to ask after an arrival time."

"Ah," said Jeeves. "Tonight."

"*In that*?" Miri twisted her free hand overhead, perhaps miming the storm without.

"Yes," said Jeeves, head-ball losing a bit of brightness. "In fact, if you will permit, we – that is, the Tree and myself, with the cat clans, have a request to put before the House."

Val Con turned his head and caught Miri's eye over his shoulder. He raised an eyebrow. She wrinkled her nose.

He turned back to Jeeves.

"Please continue," he said politely.

"Yes," Jeeves said again. "It would be good, for the House and for projects undertaken by those of the House which date before, even well before, our removal to Surebleak – if we might welcome guests. Soon. Tonight, in fact. It would be good if a guesting suite, or several, might be made ready for use."

Once again, Val Con surveyed the room, and the cats therein. Inside his head, he heard Miri laughing wryly. He felt a bump against his knee, and looked down, to find that they were surrounded by cats, tails held high, purring, and bumping.

"Tonight?" Miri's voice did not hide her wonderment. Talizea shrieked laughter at the circling felines, and Val Con asked.

"How many, and who?"

"I believe at least two, but, given the weather, there may be more. As to who they are – I do not believe we have a permissive agreement to share that information. Formerly, we have had a coded arrangement. I speak of that pair of guests. The others, if there are others, will be with us as storm-wrack. Travelers in need."

Val Con was silent. Miri was silent. Talizea was purring at a cat.

"Of course," Jeeves said, somewhat desperately, "I would not expect the House to admit these persons without knowing who they are. Indeed, as House Security, I would advise strongly against it. I will secure permission to reveal their identities."

Val Con took a deep breath.

"Is this not a great muddle, Jeeves?" he asked.

"It is, sir," Jeeves acknowledged. "Without speaking out of turn, sir, I believe I've not seen such a comprehensive muddle for some time. If you like, I will prepare a list of the ten greatest Korval muddles…."

Miri burst out laughing.

"Very good," Val Con said evenly. "You will send me the list at your leisure, perhaps with an explanation of the communication methods employed by yourself, the cats, and the Tree. What I wish to know, now, with storm-guests approaching, is: What has produced *this particular* muddle now?"

"Again sir, if I may be so bold – imminence is the problem, the *now* of *now* if you will. Imminence and commitment."

Miri straightened up, and stepped to Val Con's side, shaking her head.

"I've had dyed-in-sweater sad sack troops who couldn't've done that good playing a delay," she said, possibly to Jeeves, possibly to her lifemate.

Possibly to the cats.

Or, Val Con thought with a shiver, to the Tree.

Jeeves rolled backward a inch or two – his sometimes approximation of a bow.

"Thank you," he said gravely. "Calculation suggested that a solution to this *particular muddle* might become clear during the course of our discussion. Sadly, it has not."

"As I mentioned, the difficulty is that between us, the Tree and myself have had to deal with a range of things that are, or might be, imminent. We have discovered that time scales sometimes translate badly – that things which are *soon* to a cat or a human may not be – *as soon* to a logic with a long history or a Tree with a vastly longer history."

He paused.

"In short form, the Tree and I have pursued, in addition to our primary commitments to Line yos'Phelium and to Clan Korval, commitments to other communities. Other … persons.

"As you are aware, I had been much involved in the welfare of cats on Liad, and developed a network there of people with similar interests and necessities. Indeed, I was, through my independent funds and investments, the backbone of several organizations devoted to the welfare of non-humans. When it became obvious that we would be relocating away from Liad I did my best to spin-off such funds and anonymous board positions as appropriate.

"Meanwhile, of course, and honestly, well begun long before I appeared on the scene, the Tree has had on-going personal and support relationships with a variety of cat families and clans. In person the Tree has followed certain lines of cats. . ."

"Yes," Val Con said. "We had known as much. After all, there is Merlin --"

"Indeed, Merlin!" Jeeves said, perhaps too quickly. "But the Tree has not simply followed lines and clans of cats. It has also taken an interest in a line – that is one line – of humans."

Val Con stood suddenly taller; Miri shifted her weight as if centering herself.

"I don't mean to cause distress," Jeeves said suddenly. "But it should be clear that there are ripples to the Tree's effects, as ripples to my own, and then there is an interference patterns of sorts where your influence, and mine, and the Tree's, add up to unanticipated entanglements, to anticipated events becoming imminent well before they are expected, and to commitments thus coming due in a … as you say, sir, in a great muddle."

There was another pause. The head-ball wavered between orange, and yellow, and the palest of pale rose.

"What fuels this muddle now is a commitment made – too lightly, on one side – and too firmly – perhaps too firmly – on the other."

Miri looked at the settled cats, at Lizzy, curled beneath the blanket, and an additional blanket of cats.

"It's a bad storm," she said, slowly. "Are you sure they're coming in? That they haven't sheltered in town until this blows out?"

"We are certain that they are traveling to us now," said Jeeves. "In addition to what they hold was our promise, they labor under a constraint of time."

"Hm. And what's the Tree doing, while you and us're taking care of the hard stuff?"

"The Tree's concentration is much divided," Jeeves began – and stopped.

A dozen or more cats shifted, sat up, stood and stared at one wall of the house as if hearing something beyond the ken of human ears just beyond.

"There is a problem," Jeeves said. "Lives may be in danger. Somewhere on the road. The Tree – "

But Val Con and Miri, and Talizea too, felt the green presence now, looming and concerned, no hint of amusement in the unease, no hint of surety. Images of dragons, struggling against some unknown problem, failing to take flight, wilting, collapsing, followed by anguish and despair.

Cats began to gather, to move toward the door, to move down the hall, alert. Val Con was sure he heard a cat's complaint, strangely distant – the memory, perhaps of such a complaint, voiced by no cat present.

"The Tree is a private person," said Jeeves, "and there are promises at risk."

The green glow suffusing human thoughts receded. From without the sound of the wind increased, and with it the intermittent rumble of snow arriving in great lumps at the base of the Tree, having collected and slid down the network of branches.

ACT FOUR
Scene One

Comes a stranger from the storm
Enter Boss Gotta

Vertu's concentration was threatening to bring on a headache, the snow was bright, nearly blue in the lights. There was something else at work, too, a kind of green undertone urging her to hurry, as if the top of the hill beckoned with promises of warmth, comfort, food, bed –

"Slow!"

There was command in the girl's voice. The dog whined, and the child said, "*Malda, malda*," and other words in that language that slipped so easily by Vertu's ears.

However, she *had* slowed, in response to the tone of command, which had seemed also to speak to that green urging, which felt stronger now – closer, perhaps – but not nearly so focused on speed.

"Something happened here," Anna said, "something – look!"

Whatever *had* happened was a story told by patterns in the snow. Vertu had been following the path broken by some previous vehicle, and here *right here* there were mounds as if the wakes of two boats had solidified around some uncharted island.

The weaker track came from what may or may not have been the road to the top, the stronger veered around and …

"Fool grocery truck almost hit somebody else, right here," was Yulie's guess from the back seat. "They weren't so lucky as us – slid all over the place – maybe got kicked off-course."

"Very slow, please. We must know..."

That was Anna again, her voice strong and sure.

"See, this track, not as wide as the truck, goes this way."

Wind buffeted them with renewed strength, snow pelted the side windows, offering the track Anna pointed to as a better choice.

Vertu reluctantly let the taxi come to a stop, lights flashing, trying to analyze what she saw on the road and then, closing her eyes and finding not the expected darkness but a kind of green glow beneath her eyelids. She peered through the flow with eyes closed, trying to *see* the Tree, to orient herself, and to make a plan – preferably a plan that would not further endanger her passengers, the taxi, or herself.

If she took the left track, she would be aiming to the left of where she felt the Tree stood. If she took the right, she would be too far to the right. In this new snow-bound geography, there was no center road straight up the hill to Korval's house and Tree. Though there should be.

There should.

"We must go this way," Anna said, tapping the window insistently, and when Vertu opened her uncertain eyes she felt that perhaps *yes*, that track *might* be fresher. The certainty on the girl's tongue, though, that needed checking …

"Can you tell me if this is a wizard's call, or a guess? Are you *dramliza*?"

Anna turned her head, peering into the back seat as if for guidance.

Mary's voice was gentle.

"Anna, are you *very* sure?"

"This is the way," the girl insisted, "the Old One is worried, and –"

She turned suddenly to face Vertu.

"*You* see, Miss Vertu. Y*ou see* the Old One, I can tell. *I see* the Old One, waiting and worried. Someone – somewhere nearby – is in pain, I see them, too. Another is filled with anticipation, I have some training… we need to go this way."

Vertu closed her eyes briefly, the green presence closer, insistent. The Old One. Korval's Tree. She saw it in her mind's eye, and felt it *return her regard*, know her warmly as a familiar watcher.

When she opened her eyes the taxi was already moving. Carefully she guided it along the narrow path, snow crunching under the tires, using the vague snow-filled ruts of the previous passage as a guide.

"Hurry," Anna said, but there was no *hurry* here, off the main road and with conditions uncertain. The green presence also demanded hurry – and abruptly acquiesced to Vertu's certainty that she must go slow, and be vigilant.

There!

A flash of something blue, gone in the snow, then another, ahead.

Vertu hit the horn in warning against a car coming their way, but there was only…

A red flash, this time, closer, wilder, maybe too high to be a car, though maybe…

Rascal barked a sharp warning.

Anna cried, "Watch out!"

And Yulie said, "She's frozen!"

How Yulie knew the figure in the bright orange wrap, holding lights over her head, was female Vertu didn't ask. She was too much concerned with stopping the cab safely, and shoving the door open into the swirling snow.

"We see you! Safety is here!" she called out in Liaden – and had no time to wonder why *that* language *here* before she was answered in the same tongue.

"They're trapped! I need help, they're trapped! Follow me!"

The voice *was* female, the Liaden pure in Command mode.

The figure turned and fled away into the snow, flashing the light at them over her shoulder.

Swearing in Liaden, Vertu threw herself into the driver's seat, slammed the door, and put the cab into gear, following the high-definition boot tracks, and the occasional flash of a red or blue light through the sheeting snow.

"She says they're trapped," she told her passengers over the storm. "That they need help."

"Well, it's happenin' on our side of the toll-booth," Yulie said lightly. "Looks like we're Boss Gotta. Let's go fetch!"

Scene Two

On a snow-filled road, under a snowy sky

Rascal bounded into the snow as soon as Anna pushed the door open, following the Liaden woman's trail up to a roadside where the tire ruts disappeared off the lighted edge and down a hill.

"There!"

Vertu, Anna, Mary and Rascal stood on that edge for a moment, peering into a snow-swirled scene confused by flashing lights beneath the still accumulating crystalline surface. The woman was floundering down the hill in her light reflecting coat– soon followed by Vertu.

The car – one of the blue and red-striped cabs prone to stealing fares – was on a steep incline, tail end lower than front, driver-side mostly in the clear, while the passenger side was nearly buried in a snowdrift-covered pile of leafless brush.

Yulie arrived, and without preamble followed the trail the women had broken. He carried a bag in one hand and turned –

"Anna, you stay up there, this could be too deep for you. Mary – you come down and gimme a hand."

"You'll need me if someone's hurt!" Anna voice barely made it through the racket of the snow and wind. She was holding two of Vertu's emergency lights. Rascal charged down the hill after Yulie, casting bounding shadows.

"We need the light from up there! Stay up there and hold 'em steady! If somebody's hurt, we'll bring 'em to you!"

Vertu caught up to the woman as they both reached the side of the snowbound car; she saw a determined red face under a hood. The woman spoke, her first words taken by the wind as its toll, then –

"… blood on the driver, which I wrapped, a leg injury," the woman said, the accent of Solcintra strong . "There is some damage to the foot, also. He cannot walk, I think. And Chelada – she is in the back, unharmed – but she is pregnant and ready tonight!"

The angle made getting the door open difficult, and the chaos of the interior was not what Vertu had expected.

In the back was *not* a woman with a fat belly, but a large multi-colored cat in a travel wagon partly covered by a small rug, wide-eyed and panting. The driver-side front seat was empty, with the floor partly filled with legs stretched from the passenger side. The passenger – or driver it must be! – was awkwardly placed, leaning half on the passenger door and half on the worn seat, bent in a way meant to take strain off of a leg but clearly uncomfortable.

"We stopped on the edge," the Liaden explained to Vertu, as the others gathered to see what could be done, "then the accident with the leg. When I got out to find help, the wind slammed the door shut; the car slipped off the edge. The snow kept it from sliding too far – but this is far enough!"

"Can't walk, I don't think," the driver was saying to Yulie. "Can't stay, either. Prolly only got half-hour more heat –"

"Right. Gotta a notion to haul you outta there. That's first. Then we'll work out how to get you to the top. Here –"

There came the rustle of a bag being opened, and Yulie spoke again.

"Miss Vertu, you're smallest. We'll get you in there _"

"I'm smaller," the other woman said sharply in Terran.

"You already been in a wreck, saved this fella's life, I'm thinking, then went for a hike inna snowstorm, looking for help. Why not let the rest of us get some work in while you take a rest?"

The woman looked inclined to argue still. Mary touched her arm.

"You could do it, no one doubts," she said. "But we are fresher; the work will go quicker, and speed is important, for the cat, and the man."

The stiff shoulders relaxed somewhat.

"Yes."

"All right, then," said Yulie. "Miss Vertu, you climb on in. First thing is to get the cat into this bag. You hand her out to this lady, and then we'll have enough room to work this fella 'round so we can pull him out with these."

These were blankets pulled from the bag he'd been carrying, still bundled in their sales wrap. He shredded the thin strips in his rush, jammed them in his pocket and handed one to Vertu as she climbed over the door sill.

Rascal began barking, and jumped back from the car, barking again as snow fell from an overhead branch – and again as the car moved, threatening to slide between two of the snow-covered brush piles it leaned against.

"Right," said Yulie. "Best get to work."

Scene Three

A Rescue

In the end they stashed most of what Yulie, Mary, and Anna had brought with them into the stricken cab to make room for the rescued. With Yulie as center lead, Vertu on the right side, and Mary on the left, they managed to get the impromptu travois, and the driver, over the edge and into Vertu's cab.

The Liaden woman – Toragin, she named herself – carried a small bag in addition to the one with the quiet cat in it – led the way up the hill with Rascal a presence to her left, managing a steady pace despite the uncertain footing and wind. She accepted Anna's hand as an aid to getting over the edge and stood there, cuddling her cat and her bag.

Once over the edge, the travois team took a moment to rest. The wounded cab driver was swearing softly and constantly, and Vertu moved slightly away from him, so as to give him the privacy such a rendering of art deserved.

That put her close to Toragin, who was also speaking – not swearing, Vertu thought, but alternating between murmuring comforting phrases to the cat, and recriminating with someone else – or perhaps herself.

"You told her she would have her kittens under branch. A promise given, and cast away, with no word or care for her. As if you had forgotten!"

"All right," Yulie called. "All's we got left is the easy part!"

Mary laughed, and took hold of her side of the blanket. Vertu stepped up, and took hold of hers.

They reached Vertu's cab, all the worse for the weather, and the rescue. When the passenger's side front door was opened to urge Toragin and Chelada into the warmth, Rascal settled onto the floor at her feet.

The rest of them dealt with the driver, the final configuration being Yulie, Mary, and Anna sitting together on the back seat with the driver half reclining across their laps. His boots were in Anna's lap, and Vertu saw her nod with satisfaction as Mary twisted to pull the cab's first aid kit from the compartment under the seat.

Meanwhile, Toragin was next to Vertu, a blanket wrapped around her coat, barely looking up as the heavily burdened cab got cautiously under way. The bag was in her lap, open, and she was looking down at the cat curled there. Rascal sat very quietly, crowded against Toragin's legs as if offering warmth, alert ears and face turned respectfully away from the cat, whose back was turned to him.

Vertu measured her turn, looking to the end of the road, as determined by the marks their boots and Rascal's wandering pace had left.

"If you see something outside I should know about," she said to her passengers at large, "please tell me. Elsewise talk as you need, but not to me, is that understood? I will need to concentrate."

Those in the back answered in the affirmative, while next to her the mumbling continued, low enough that it did not distract. From the back seat, Anna spoke low and with composure.

"I will unwrap these wet towels and inspect your hurts. Now, tell me – this part here?"

"It stings."

"If I do this ..."

"Don't *touch* it, it already ..."

"To help, I need to work in two ways. One way will hurt to start, since your muscles have tangled up their needs with your pain. Also, you have been pierced by something, but we'll need to have good light to see that. We will leave the wrap in place."

"I will touch the muscles and warm them some, and they will be able to relax, some. When they do the other muscles will fight – don't kick! If you need, Mary will hold your hand – squeeze that if you hurt, but don't twist away. So, open your hands and let Mary have one..."

Vertu followed the ruts back to the proper road where the ghost tracks of passed vehicles could barely be searched out in the lights.

"You want to go right just here," Yulie said from the backseat. "Not too sharp, 'cause it might be best to miss where the other tracks was. I'm thinking there'll be a rock pile kind of shining off the side in your lights, 'cause the snow's going cold and fine now so we can see better. Come summer there's a spring near that rock, so sometimes we get a squiggly slick spot in winter if the ditch catches freewater."

He was right, of course, about missing the tracks, and the news about the potential ice was useful.

Vertu drove, saw the rock face, felt the small lurch as the traveled over one ice stream, and another, and another. She just let the cab find its own way through, and when they were through the worst of, she touched the accelerator gently.

"Relax that spot now," Anna said to her reluctant patient. "Yes, you can. I will touch you here and you'll feel the spot. I will rub it and we'll let the muscles relax, they are as tight as if you stood on tip toe – and you do not. Yes, see, when I touch the warm will help you relax… very good. Now it doesn't hurt as bad, and it will hurt less soon."

"Going to hurt awhile," came the reply … "that's my driving foot, you know! If I don't drive I can't eat!"

"Tonight you'll eat, and tomorrow," came the soothing voice, "and after that, too, I'm sure. "Driving is only delayed a few days..."

"Here then, hold your glove. I will try to see if there's anything more wrong – squeeze hard if you need ..."

"Sleet, sleet, sleet!"

"Squeeze and be a little quiet – Miss Vertu needs to concentrate!"

Gloves made Vertu recall the other new passenger. She glanced to that side, noting that cat and bag had been tucked into the floor, between the woman's boots; Rascal sitting firmly on the door side of those same boots.

"Toragin, your name is?" Vertu murmured. "Toragin was a Lazmeln name some generations ago, if I recall my lineages properly."

"And is now," the woman admitted, "though for how long is a guess. I am Toragin del'Pemridj Clan Lazmeln."

"Whatever your line, Toragin, you might take your gloves off now, and open your coat. This car is not so cold as the other, and the gloves will be holding cold. Your boots may hold some cold, too, but I have the heat up – as well as I may and still see the road – on feet."

The young woman divested herself of her gloves, doing her best not to disturb the cat in the footwell.

"You sound of Solcintra," she ventured. "You are?"

Vertu glanced at the passenger wryly.

"The Council of Clans made it possible for me to find work on Surebleak – and on Surebleak I am Vertu Dysan."

"Ah," said the knowing tone. "And Vertu was at least twice a name in a line in Solcintra." After a short pause and a glance at Vertu she went on, "I cannot put my clan in debt for this rescue, I fear, but Chelada and I both See you, Vertu Dysan, and somewhere there will be Balance for your timely assistance."

Vertu made a short motion with her hand – a Surebeak usage of a pilot's shorthand –

"Call this neighbor-work, Toragin. You would have done the same for me..."

Neighbor work – well, that was more properly a Surebleak thing than a Liaden one as well.

"I have no such connection," Toragin said, "Those I know here to recognize are some of Korval, and of course, the Tree beyond Korval's gate, and whoever else has shied away without formal notice, of whom there are many, I'm told. I *had been* neighbor to the Tree until it was chased away by the Council of Clans."

Vertu reconciled the map in her head now with the memory of fares delivered in years past, and indeed Lazmeln's clan house was – had been –in the physical shadow of the Tree.

Silence for a moment or two then, which Vertu was glad of as the cab skittered on some unseen unevenness below the snowy surface.

The silence gave way then to a cooing noise.

Toragin had taken the purring cat into her lap and was speaking in cat-like tones, expertly petting and perhaps stroking a flank or belly. The purr fell into a breathy pant; Toragin's posture changed as she became more alert.

Vertu did an extra scan of the road; but saw nothing that might have claimed the other woman's attention. Instead Toragin carefully placed the cat into the bag at her feet, staring into the darkness there.

"Is it this close to your time then?" Toragin's voice was low. "I think I feel contractions, Chelada!"

"Here! Yulie, hand this up to the front! The cat has need!"

Anna was moving things and at that sound there was rustling behind Vertu's head and then:

"Toragin, that's right – take this."

This was a mostly dry blanket of bright green, threaded over the seat tops …

"She will not wait, or cannot," Anna said. "Help her make a better nest for her four."

"Let Rascal come back here with us," said Mary. "There's room on the floor, and another blanket."

Anna spoke in that other language. In the screen, Vertu saw the dog carefully jump to the seat-top and then over, into Mary's arms. Anna reached out to tug an ear, and then down he went to the floor and his own blanket.

Vertu sped the cab up just a little, wishing she had a better idea of where they were.

ACT FIVE

In the Hall of the Mountain King

The ruckus room had the air now of a council of war, with Jeeves reporting on results of scans borrowed from ships in orbit and aircraft in flight, of radio waves interpreted and – "There are two cabs thought to be on the road between here and the city proper; one driven by Vertu Dysan, carrying Yulie Shaper and other fares to his home. The other is a wild cab which may be carrying one or more passengers from *Finifter's Shave,"* Jeeves said. "It seems that the passengers of both cabs have consolidated, and that the House may be called upon to host eight, of whom five are known. We have not yet received permission to reveal the names of the remaining three, though this is perhaps imminent, as one of the principals has taken up recriminations."

"Recriminations against the Tree?" Val Con murmured. "How could such a thing be so?"

"The Tree has erred, Master Val Con. It feels its error, keenly."

"Gotta admit, that's something new and innerestin," Miri said.

"Perhaps not entirely new, though I allow it to be a rarity," Val Con answered, and looked to Jeeves.

"The nature of these *recriminations* interests me. Do they presage violence against the Tree, or, indeed, the House? Is Korval considered a party to this – error?"

"The Tree is attempting to ascertain the answers to these very questions," Jeeves said.

"The travelers, as I understand, have been having an adventure, and the Tree is not acclimated to carrying on communications – conversations – with those not of Jela's Line, especially not at a distance, when the communicant is distraught. The Tree does not *know* this individual, merely is *aware* of them as a … closely affiliated ally."

"Or even as a one of a number of carefully engineered guard pets," Val Con murmured.

"You are unfair, sir," Jeeves said, chidingly. "Also, I would suggest that the Tree finds itself in a unique situation, which it is working to understand, and to resolve in such a manner that all parties are satisfied – and safe. This is perhaps not the time to distract it with more recrimination."

"You are quite correct," Val Con said. "I am insupportably rude. I withdraw my tasteless irony until such time as the Tree and myself are less dismayed by the imminent arrival of a stranger who may wish to visit harm on my lifemate and our child."

"Thank you, sir. Your understanding is appreciated."

Miri snorted. Val Con sighed, and reached over to take her hand. They were occupying the pillow corner, sitting crosslegged atop the blanket, cats in various attitudes of alertness and repose scattered about. Talizea had been sent up to the nursery, accompanied by a guard of six, Mrs. pel'Esla having been directed to allow the cats to sleep with the heir, if they, and she, so desired.

"I wonder," Val Con said now, "if you will hazard a guess as to the Tree's core problem with this recriminating individual? I understand that we are looking at approximation rather than exactitude."

"Yes," said Jeeves, head ball glowing and pulsing in shades of orange. "It is my understanding that the Tree is dealing with the weight of … guilt."

"Guilt?" Miri's startled response beat Val Con's by a quarter second.

"Yes. It has lately been expressing concern over decisions made long ago. The severing of Tinsori Light's last link to the crystallized universe inspired a great deal of thought, of what might be called introspection, as if there had been a tension for centuries between the great resistance and the smaller deeds. Now that there is no great resistance to be concerned with, the importance of small deeds becomes magnified."

A pause. The head ball flickered.

"Guilt. Remorse. Regret – I have only analogs to work from, you understand, because the Tree's sentience is not like yours, or mine, and it encompasses far more that we can comprehend. Simply put – now that the great resistance has collapsed, the Tree considers what it might have done – differently."

"So it's depressed," Miri said.

"Possibly," said Jeeves. "The analogs –"

"Yes," said Val Con. "We deal in approximations. It is not so uncommon, when a large, all-consuming project has finally seen completion, to experience a sense of – disorientation, even sadness. A sense, perhaps, that victory ought to have been something – *more*."

"Healer?" Miri murmured.

"If so, it would need to be one of us, who grew up under branch – and received the – pardon me, the *benefits* of the Tree's long interaction with our bloodlines."

Miri looked thoughtful.

"Tree's really old," she commented. "Maybe the Clutch could help?"

"That," said Jeeves, "is a useful thought. Collectively, the Clutch elders may be as old in this universe as the Tree was in the Crystal Universe. There is no adequate or useful comparison of age, but the Clutch sentience is far closer to the Tree's than to human sentience – or the sentience of an Independent Logic designed by humans."

"We ought also to consider the norbears, in that wise," said Val Con. "Perhaps we ought consult a counsel of elders."

"Clutch, norbears, Tree, Free Logics, humans." Miri was shaking her head. "Would that include Uncle?"

Val Con lifted his eyes to the ceiling as if seeking an answer to that question, then returned his gaze to Jeeves.

"*Do* we need a Healing? Or a council of elders?"

Jeeves' head ball dimmed somewhat, signaling deep thought.

"I believe we do not, in the short term, need either. An *informal* council of elders is an idea deserving consideration. Such a council might have understood the problem of the Department much sooner. Given open information, such a council might have managed an answer to Tinsori Light as well, but such openness would not come easily."

Miri wrinkled her nose. Val Con shook his head.

"We shall place the council of elders aside just now. For the moment, what is required in order to honor the Tree's ambition to resolve the present situation in a manner that is both satisfactory and safe for all?"

"I –" Jeeves began, and stopped, head ball flashing red, then returning to orange.

"Lord Pat Rin calls via relay," he announced. "He asks first for the Road Boss. May I put him through?"

"Of course. Here if you will."

Miri joined Val Con at the com screen. Pat Rin was there before them, his smile wry. "My immediate need is for the Road Boss, but I also have a brief question for the delm: The next time the clan requires rescue will you please find me a clement planet to suborn?"

"The delm," said Miri, "is sitting undertree in the puckerbrush in a stay-don't-move blizzard. The delm chooses to smile gently at your levity..."

"Yes, I suppose they do. I thank the delm, most sincerely, for their forbearance."

He gave a casual pilot's hand sign – *next order of business* – "I have news from Mr. McFarland that Vertu Dysan is in the midst of a rescue and wishes to stop, with her passengers, and shelter at Jelaza Kazone for the evening, given the difficulty of driving. I gather contact is intermittent in this storm. Also, I'm informed that at least one of the seven passengers insists the Tree itself has issued an invitation."

"Heard a rumor like that ourselves," Miri said. "Tree's not being all that communicative right now."

She heard Val Con's agreement inside her head before she saw his nod.

"Rooms are being prepared," he said. "Pass that along if you get contact back. Otherwise, we are forewarned, and the gate will be open for them."

"Excellent. I expect that we will speak again in the morning. Luck willing, we will not have to speak again, tonight."

The contact ended, screen now showing a view from the spaceport – the packet ship *Finifter's Shave* bathed in bright lights as snow drifted and blustered across the tarmac and receded into darkness.

Weather aside, there was a silence in the ruckus room as the humans looked one to another, and it appeared the cats as well. Then a cat made a brief sound, and shared it again, as did another, and soon there was an undercurrent of restless feline muttering – never quite so formal as *meow* nor as quiet as *prrt* – as the gathered cats mustered themselves into a company before splitting into tribes and leaving on their own business.

"Is it possible, Jeeves, that you might get the Tree's attention? I ask since Miri and I will shortly settle ourselves down and consider the Tree until it considers us. The Tree must understand that whatever its past misdeeds, we must talk, and talk now, before our guests arrive."

ACT SIX

Scene One

Exploring Inner Landscapes

Toragin was not flustered. Say rather that she was anxious. Or perhaps it was beyond that, to something more personal and more powerful. She was, in fact, bordering on that strange cliff between awe and frustration that breeds a righteous – well, she wasn't supposed to feel the stress that bordered on anger. Not. Supposed. To.

She'd felt Chelada's contractions, and was familiar enough with the process; getting the dog out of the way and the blanket down made things easier, but still, here she was having what must stand for an adventure, on a world she'd never heard of before Korval's Tree had gone away. She was not an adventurer. She did not *believe in* adventures.

But she *did* believe in promises.

Promises? Oh, she'd had promises from her grandmother, who knew that Toragin's barely socially acceptable "not of the usual-type" was something the Healers would not Heal and the matchmakers never bothered to challenge. The promise to "let the child do worthy work and have her cats" … oh, *that* promise had covered pregnant cats and feral, that promise had covered mystery organizations sending cat food and cat-vets around Liad and even to Lowport – but now? Here was the result of that promise to let the child be who she was … and Chelada's labor was within moments of producing her first kitten in the midst of dangerous weather on a dangerous world, when she had been promised the comfort and safety of birthing those kittens beneath the Tree's very branches.

Chelada had earned that promise. Toragin had earned the right to be taken seriously. Or so she had thought. Now it appeared that, yet again, she had no rights in the face of another's necessity. That – was such a constant in her life, she had scarcely noticed the slight.

But Chelada.

Chelada had been *promised*, and Toragin had stood witness to that promise.

So, when it came apparent that Chelada *would* have kittens, Toragin had done research – she was good at research – found the new location of the Tree, transit time, cost, and only then told her delm of the necessity of taking Chelada to the place where she might redeem her promise.

Her delm had asked a few perfunctory questions about the potential of a secret lover having gone to ground on Surebleak, and had authorized purchase of the tickets, one way, with the understanding that a return fare would come from Toragin's quartershare. She had also acquiesced to the demands of the nadelm, who had "grave misgivings" about Toragin's ability to travel alone, and called in the Healer who was most familiar with Toragin's case.

To him, Toragin had said, "Yes, Chelada is pregnant and bears a promise from the great Tree of Korval. Her kittens are to be born under – they *must be born under* – the Tree's protection."

The Healer had bowed. It was, he said, apparent that Toragin believed this to be true to the very base of her being. The cat's claim on the Tree was not as accessible as the cat's claim on Toragin, and Toragin's on the cat, but he allowed such claims, also, to be true, and strong. The Tree's claim on Toragin was a matter for some consideration. Was it a child's fascination grown into a obsession? Was it a child's fancy grown into compulsion? If it was either, ought it to be Healed?

The Healer thought not. The Healer, and the Hall, found the Tree disquieting. If Toragin were "Tree-mazed," said the Healer, best she was left to sort it out on her own. And if the method of sorting out was a trip to Surebleak and a confrontation, that was surely for the best.

And now, here she was – *not* under the branches of the Tree, and Chelada giving birth, not safe, but in appalling danger.

Though, they must be nearby. She could – well, *hear* was scarcely accurate. Not like she could *hear* the cats. But she felt attention on her, caught nuance, and she spoke to it, careful to keep her voice low, so as not to disturb the driver's concentration.

"I hear you hiding in the wind. Is this your storm? Is this to deny us? I am here. Chelada is here. We come to claim the boon you have promised since first I saw your glow! Show yourself!"

Chelada made a small sound, just then, a small sound. In the blanket, a form expanded into the strange world.

"Listen," said Toragin sharp and low, "your cats are coming. Show yourself!"

Yes. The fluster was gone, anxiety was gone, and now there was no boundary or border about it. Anger it was, and it flared.

"Think of something besides yourself. Think about those whose lives depend on your whim!"

In the dimness she felt the presence, felt a confused contrition. The presence receded slightly, returned, offering a sense of warmth, perhaps of hope, reminiscent of the first time she'd stared out her window into the silhouetted shadow of the Tree and demanded that it see her.

Patience, she felt she heard from the night. *You will be safe. You will be satisfied.*

And then, so understated that she suspected she had not heard it at all.

Please forgive me.

Scene Two

In the shadow of the Tree

Snow on the windscreen flashed with the bright glow of lightning inside the storm. Again and now, thunder rolled over the cab, echoing. A bolt of lightning struck close to the car, a weird green glow behind it all, the combination of flashes and sound so overwhelming that Vertu eased the cab to a halt.

Thunder died away, yet the wind-driven snow remained too thick to see through as the car shook. The passengers said nothing for several minutes, listening to Toragin's coos and the cat's undernoises when they could be heard over the storm's constant rumble.

Vertu, fearing for alertness, recalled the coffee and, with it, the food.

"I cannot see to drive at this moment. I can share some food, if you can take coffee – "

Toragin had water for her and the cat. She declined coffee but accepted a half-handwich; the others were pleased to get something – the recumbent driver in the back being allowed to partially sit up to sip at one of the cups passed to the rear seat.

Amid thanks and sips it took a moment for Vertu to realize that the cab's wind-inspired trembling had nearly stopped; indeed, the snow was no longer falling slantwise. Her cab's lights gained range, though how much was hard to gauge in the soft-edged whiteness.

"Might be over!" Yulie said, startling everyone else in the near silence.

Vertu let the windscreen clean itself; now only tiny flakes fell, the density and demeanor of the storm fallen to flurry that quickly.

"Guess the lightning blew it out," suggested the other cab driver. "Must've been one last huff of wind!"

Anna spoke then, sounding as certain as a priestess:

"We are in the Old One's shadow. It knows where we are and has sucked the storm into itself!"

Despite the outside temperature, now well below frost point, Vertu lowered her window briefly, allowing a few fine crystals of flurry to drift in on a lazy clean-smelling breeze. Peering forward, up the road, she felt that she knew exactly where the Tree was.

"Ten minutes it'd be from here in dry weather," Yulie volunteered, "might be eight if you was hurrying. Guessing two or three time that now, driving careful. Do that – drive careful, 'cause it's a heckuva walk in the snow. Even if the wind's gone."

Another brilliant crystal of snow flitted into the window before Vertu sealed it.

"Three," said Toragin. "Three kittens so far. They will want a warm place to sleep tonight."

The rest of the drive was not uneventful – there was the arrival of the fourth kitten to begin with, and then there was the moment when the cab's entire structure began to glow, starting with a light misty haze and then with a vivid blueish glow that slowly phased to green.

"Salmo's Fire!" Yulie said excitedly. "Salmo's Fire happens when them electrons gets all into a plasma and settles tight around something that can trade electrons around it. I've seen it on quiet nights hanging on 'quipment tips and stuff. My brother had it ball up at the end of his rifle one night when we was out …"

Yulie let the sentence die then, like the memory might be best if left unstirred, but everyone in the cab could feel the glow dancing across their skins. Chelada's fourth kitten was born then, enveloped along with her mother in the pulsing green. Vertu felt her hair standing away from her head, and saw motion in the "fire" itself, as if the kittens were, one by one, petted and soothed by the action of the plasma, the final kitten getting an extra helping.

"I don't do much dreaming but I could think I was dreaming this whole thing!" Again Yulie caught the mood of the cab, but the glow was real, reflecting back into the vehicle from the surrounding snow for several eerie minutes until it faded infinitesimally to normal.

Vertu's glance flitted from interior to exterior, the night's darkness gaining depth as clouds rapidly dissipated; now only the instrument lights lit the interior.

The darkness outside wasn't complete since the cab's lights played over the snow covered road and the snow covered vegetation. Vertu glanced up, sensing –

Yes! There, where that glow was – *that* was where the Tree waited!

Toragin laughed. Vertu caught sight of the nursery as the new mother dabbed at the kittens, adjusting herself for their comfort. Toragin's face was bright in the instrument lights. She gasped as the pinnacle of green was briefly visible between the line of vegetation that flanked the road before it hit another curve.

"There, that's the Tree!"

"Old One!" said Anna, then something in that other language to Rascal, and perhaps to Mary, while Yulie muttered.

"'splains those pods right good. Darn thing's got eyes can see all the way to town and more, don't it?"

After a pause he went on –

"Prolly another three minutes, now, to my place. Me an' Mary, Anna an' Rascal'll just get out and walk in – no sense you going all the way in to the house, Miss Vertu, then havin' to come back out again. Been enough o'that recently. This fella here'll be better with the neighbors, and Miss Toragin and her family's got their invitation, and Miss Vertu'll do the smart thing, and let the neighbor take care of her tonight."

"Yes," said Vertu, thinking that the chances were very good, indeed, that *Clan Korval's* comms worked. She ought to call Cheever, and Jemmie. . .

"Here we're comin' up on it," Yulie said. "Just ease to a stop under that twisted tree there. Right, now –"

He stopped talking.

Vertu looked out the window, at the so-called driveway.

"That drift's taller than Anna," Mary commented. "I guess we could toss her and Rascal over it."

"Don't know how wide is it," Yulie said, sounding momentarily glum. "Not to say that leaves you an' me walking through up to our waists."

"We can do it."

"Well, sure, we *can* do it," said Yulie, rallying. "But do we *gotta* do it, that's the question."

There was a moment's silence.

"Well, no. We *ain't* gotta do it. We'll just all of us go on up the hill, if Miss Vertu'll still have us, and ask the neighbor do they have room."

He sniffed.

"Huh. Not sure where that come from. Like somebody whispered – welcome – inside my ear."

"An invitation," Toragin said surprisingly, "from the Tree. I have heard such whisperings myself."

"Guess that'll do until something official turns up," said Yulie.

Toragin gave a rueful laugh.

"Perhaps it will, at that," she said.

ACT SEVEN

In the Hall of the Mountain King
Enter Dragons

The room was full of dragons.

Given that the room in question was a small, intimate parlor off a side hall with quick access to an outside door, it might be said to have been overfull of dragons.

There were, for instance, the two curled together on the sofa near the fire. The room had been built to their scale.

There were, too, those other dragons – dozens and dozens of dragons undertaking an intricate, multi-leveled dance against a glittering sky. Wings brushed wings, dancers wheeling. Here, one or two folded and fell, wings snapping wide with a *boom* and they rocketed upward, into the dance and through it, seeking the limits of space.

Green warmth informed the dance – the Tree's regard for its dragons was true. It remembered them all, celebrated their lives and the frequent astonishment of their achievements. Mint scented the air, and Miri saw a wash of green, like leaves between her and the dancers. Beside her Val Con shifted, and she felt him move, wings stirring, as if he would rise from the sofa and join the others in celebration.

There came the impression of an indulgent laugh; the idea of a kiss upon the cheek.

The Tree embraced them, and for a moment Miri's senses swam, as she stretched her wings, feeling the starwind fill them, bearing her further up, beyond branches and leaves. She looked to her right where Val Con flew at her very wingtip.

Above them, the dance was ending; dragons peeling away from the group, singly, or in small groups, fading into the glittering sky.

Miri folded her wings, saw Val Con do the same, and opened her eyes a moment later to the fire in the hearth, her head on Val Con's shoulder, and her legs curled beneath her.

She stretched, and sat up, looking into brilliant green eyes.

"Gotta say, you're a nice lookin' dragon," she told him.

He smiled.

"I return the compliment. We should fly together again – soon."

"Done," she said and raised tipped her head, considering. The impression of a vast, green regard remained present, and also an undercurrent of what might have been – apprehension.

"So," she said. "We're loved and respected and the first in the Tree's regard. I read that right?"

"I believe that is the message, yes," Val Con said. "It must of course be flattering to know that we stand at the pinnacle of the Tree's regard. However, the Tree fails to instruct us with regard to those others who are also held in its regard. It is the duty of those who stand high to care for those who stand lower. As delm, we know this."

The warm greenness lost some of its depth; Miri felt a little flutter, as if of confusion, and a quick flash of dragons, dancing. The feeling of close green attention faded, somewhat.

"If I may. . ." Jeeves' spoke from the ceiling grid.

"Please," said Val Con. "We should like to offer the promise bearer proper honor, and time, as I understand it, is short."

"Indeed, sir. The taxi has passed Yulie Shaper's house. Scans indicate that the drive is impassable. The house will be asked to guest twelve. I have updated staff."

"Twelve!" Miri repeated.

"To be precise, four of those are newly born, and will wish to stay with their mother, who will, I believe, wish to remain with the other promise-bearer. Of the six remaining, four are Yulie Shaper and his party of four – this including Rascal – one is Vertu Dysan, and the other is the driver of another taxi, who has taken injury. I calculate the car will be with us in seven minutes."

"Time is very short," Val Con said dryly. "Jeeves – sum up, if you will!"

"Yes, sir. In short – the recent opening of the Tree's horizons, including conversations with various members of the Clutch, access to the Surebleak gestalt, has resulted in the Tree re-evaluating the way it communicates with all of us. As I said before, the Tree realizes that it has made errors in the past. Some – I would say, most – of those errors are so far in the past that the Tree can do nothing to rectify them. It has understood that it must Balance with the promise-bearers now approaching, that to do anything else would be to dishonor the long service of its dragons. This realization, combined with the broadening of its understanding, brought additional introspection. It has become aware that, while it has acted always for the good of Jela's heirs, that – occasionally – it may have worked with too much force, acted with, I will say, *hauteur* –"

The feeling of intense green attention was back, so dense Miri worried that the walls might crack.

"Yes," said Jeeves, "hauteur. The Tree will be making changes in the way it deals with Jela's get – that is a promise, a *considered promise*. It will also seek to modify and improve its way of dealing with those others who may assist, or serve it in capacity outside the care of dragons."

He paused; Miri caught the sense that he was listening.

"Yes. The Tree offers the idea that its dragons are – family, sir. And that the promise-bearers, and those others which assist it in the pursuit of its hobbies are – friends."

There was a strong sense of affirmation inside the little room – the flames fluttered, as if by a sudden draft. Then the sense of the Tree was gone entirely, and Jeeves spoke once more.

"The cab is here. I have opened the gate to them."

"Excellent," Val Con said, rising with Miri. "We will meet them at the side door. Please have Nelirikk attend us. If our wounded cabbie cannot walk, then he can be carried, and given medical attention."

ACT EIGHT

Scene One

The Gate

Enter Nelirikk and Jarome

Something glittered in the headlights. The cab crept forward, out of deep snow into what felt like naked road surface beneath the wheels. The glitter resolved itself into a gate – *the* gate, wrought metal with leaves and dragons woven along the bars and arches.

Vertu sighed; heard it echoed by every one of her passengers, save, perhaps, the kittens.

"Made it," said Yulie. "Wasn't never any doubt, not with Miss Vertu drivin'."

She felt laughter tighten her chest, rising, and deliberately swallowed. Perhaps it was wisest to not laugh *yet*, she thought.

For a long moment, they sat there, contemplating the gate, while the gate contemplated them.

Slowly, then, the sections separated, swinging back with a stately inevitability. Vertu nudged the cab forward, noting that the driveway beyond the gate was in fact clear of snow.

Carefully, she followed the drive, and when snow again appeared on the surface, she scrupulously kept the cab to the dry surface until the drive ended at a low wall, a lighted door beyond.

Standing between them and the door were three people in snow coats – two Liaden high, and one very tall – one of Korval's guards, she knew, but was uncertain as to which, with his face hidden in the shadow of his hood.

"There, now, driver," said Yulie, apparently to the wounded cabbie. "That big fella there, that's Nelirikk. He'll have you outta here and them legs looked at and fixed up before you can say *snowflakes are fallin' on my head*!"

"He a medic?" asked the cabbie, sounding nervous.

"He was a soldier, now security for the Road Bosses," Mary said surprisingly. "He is a field medic, and Anna has already done much of what was needful for you. I think you will find that you can drive, tomorrow."

"That'd be fine by me," said the cabbie. "S'long's I can get my cab out."

"You come on over to my place tomorrow, after we're all rested," Yulie said. "Get the snow tractor out and rustle up a couple o'my hands. Haver out in no time."

Vertu locked the wheel, opened the door, and got out of the cab.

The three walked forward, and Vertu recognized Korval Themselves.

She bowed, lesser to greater, and received bows of welcome to the guest in return.

"Boss," she said, in Terran so that all of her fares would understand what she asked for in their behalf. "The storm brought us to you. We ask shelter, and rest –"

"And Rascal wants his dinner!" Anna called out, opening the back door and coming to Vertu's side, dog at her heel.

"Good even, Miri. Good even, Val Con. Nelirikk, come and get Jarome out of the back. He's hurt, and needs to be looked at in good light."

"Good evening, Anna. Rascal," said Val Con yos'Phelium.

"Have you done first aid?" Nelirikk asked Anna.

"I'll show you, but first you need to get him out."

"Yes," he said, and walked around Vertu, heading for the back of the car.

"There's Yulie and Mary, too, we heard," said Miri Tiazan. "And someone with a cat and kittens."

"I am here, Korval."

The front passenger door opened, and Toragin stepped out. She advanced, and bowed as one who has been invited.

"Toragin del'Pemridj Clan Lazmeln, Chelada is with me, and her newborns. She was promised by the Tree itself that she would have her kittens safe beneath its branches."

"And so the Tree is forsworn," said Val Con yos'Phelium. "We may have you escorted directly to the Tree, with Chelada and the newborn, if that is your wish."

"Yes," said Toragin, and paused as a burst of cursing at the back of the cab told the progress of Cabbie Jarome's extraction.

"I will need a basket, or a box," Toragin said, turning back to Korval. "Right now, the kittens and Chelada are on the floor, in a blanket."

"Right," said Miri Tiazan, and tipped her head. "Jeeves, need us some kitten transport."

"Yes, Miri," a mellow voice spoke from the air. "I will bring it."

There came another burst of swearing, and a gasp. Rascal barked, once, and here came Nelirikk, Anna and the dog beside him, Jarome flung over one broad shoulder in a field carry.

The door opened as they approached, and they vanished within. A moment later, a man-high cylindrical object, with a bright orange ball where a man's head might have been exited by the same door, holding a basket in one gripper, and a blanket in the other.

It approached and extended the basket.

"Will these suffice?"

Toragin considered. The basket was deep and wide enough for all five cats. The blanket would make a soft nest.

"Thank you," she said. "I will be a moment."

She turned back to the cab.

From the back of the cab now came Yulie and Mary. They passed Toragin, and approached, Yulie with a grin on his face.

"Some kinda storm," he said affably. "Get 'em like that at the old home?"

"Nothing nearly so awe-inspiring," Val Con yos'Phelium said. "I see that you have come to no harm."

"Not the least bit," Yulie said. "We're a might peckish, though. I don't s'pose there's any of Mrs. ana'Tak's cookies 'round the kitchen?"

"In fact, there is an entire buffet in the breakfast room. Mrs. ana'Tak would have it no other way. I believe there are cookies, and also soup, and biscuits, wine and juice. If you will, let us show you the way."

He turned, sweeping an arm out toward the patio door, ushering the couple forward.

"Vertu?" Miri Tiazan gave her a grin. "That's you, too. Got rooms ready, too, 'cause if you don't mind my sayin' so, you're lookin' all done in."

Vertu managed a smile.

"It was a trying day," she murmured.

"All done now, though, right? This way –"

She turned, and Vertu followed, pausing just at the edge of the patio to look up – up into the now-cloudless dark sky, where a monumental shadow was silhouetted against the stars.

Scene Two

In the Hall of the Mountain King
Enter Joey

There were cats. Many cats. Cats of all colors. Vertu walked carefully, unwilling to step on a vulnerable paw in her storm boots, until she saw that the cats displayed a fine understanding of where she and her boots were, and that they were not so much a random mob, as an – escort down the hall.

"Hoping to get some handouts from the buffet," Miri Tiazan said from beside her. "Hear them tell it, all they got here is empty bowls."

Vertu smiled. She had left her coat on the hook by the door, alongside her hosts' jackets, and those of Yulie and Mary. It was pleasantly warm in the hallway; she was glad to be walking, no matter the comfort of her driving seat, and the cats, seen as escort, began to amuse her.

Perhaps a little too much, she thought.

"I am grateful for the House's care," she said, in Liaden.

Miri Tiazan slanted a look at her face.

"The House is grateful, to be able to extend its care," she answered, and her accent in the High Tongue was that of Solcintra. She jerked her chin slightly to the right.

"Here we are," she said, back in Terran.

Yulie and Mary were standing, struck, in the center of the room, while Val Con yos'Phelium was seen at the wine table, seeing to the filling of glasses.

"Driver Dysan," he said, not looking 'round. "Red or white?"

"Red, if you please," she answered, as their cat escort flowed around her feet, and one in particular – a large, fuzzy gray with black feet – marched forward with purpose.

"Joey!" shouted Yulie Shaper, and went down on one knee, arms wide. Vertu thought to glance at the wine table, but Val Con yos'Phelium's nerves were as steady as any Scout's might be. The glasses were intact, the wine unspilled.

The gray cat leapt, and landed in Yulie's arms. He rose, hugging it over his shoulder.

"But, Joey, what're you doin' here? Botherin' the Bosses?"

"Not at all," said the host, turning to offer Mary a glass of the white. "We believe that several of yours came up the hill when the storm became apparent, as support for our cats in-house."

"Well, that's a nice face to put on it," said Yulie, "an' I'm glad you kept 'em inside. But they start makin' a habit – or a nuisance – you send 'em packing."

"Sure we will," said Miri Tiazan. "You ever try to tell a cat what to do?"

Mary laughed.

"Yulie, your wine," she said.

"Hmm – oh, right. Thanks, Boss."

Joey slung over one shoulder like a furry towel, Yulie turned and took his glass.

Vertu stepped forward and received hers, with a bow of the head.

"My thanks," she murmured.

"My pleasure," he returned.

"I wonder," she said then, "if I might use the comm."

"Of course. I will show you."

Jemmie was pleased, though not surprised, to learn that Vertu was sheltering at the top of the hill.

"Road boss knows their bidness, always said so," she said in sum-up.

"When I come back down," Vertu said, "we will need to talk about the rogue cabs. We nearly lost a man to his own incompetence, and a failure to maintain an adequate machine. It is our place as the professionals to do something."

"Yanno, I been thinking the same. We'll talk about it when you get back home. Might need to take it up with the Bosses – but that's later, Vertu. Right now, you call your big man an' let him know you're safe, fed, an' about to tuck up. Then you go and tuck up, hear me?"

"I hear you, Jemmie," Vertu said softly. "Thank you for your care."

"Funny to be thanked for something comes so nat'ral. Now, you hang up this call and get with that man o'yours."

#

"So, you got up to the house all right, then. They taking good care of you?"

Someone who was not as familiar with Cheever McFarland's voice might have thought him unconcerned, even bored. Vertu heard otherwise, and smiled into the phone.

"Indeed, we have arrived safely, all twelve of us."

"*Twelve* of you! How'd that happen?"

She smiled, took a sip of her wine, and told him.

Sometime during the telling, she felt something soft land in her lap and glanced down to find one of the ubiquitous cats sitting on one knee and kneading the other, while purring. Loudly.

"What's that, a motor?"

"A cat," Vertu told him. "This house is full of cats, and apparently this one has seen an opportunity to claim a comfortable lap for itself."

"What color cat?" Cheever asked.

Vertu frowned.

"All the colors," she said, after a moment. "Brown, orange, grey, white, black… The two front feet are white; the two back feet are black."

"Got a real looker, there," Cheever said. "So, what're you gonna do about the wild cabs?"

Vertu laughed. He knew her so well.

"Jemmie and I will talk about it, when I am back home."

"Good idea. Let me know if you need any help putting together a presentation for the Bosses."

She shook her head. The cat continued to purr and knead.

"Jemmie also thought we'd have to get the Bosses involved," she said.

"Road Boss at least," said Cheever. "Might be best to bring it up to all of 'em, though. Surebleak's gonna be needing associations and formal rules sooner more'n later."

"I fear you are correct," she said, "though I would not want to see Surebleak become Liad."

"Nobody wants that!" Cheever said in mock horror. "Now, you get yourself something to eat and some downtime. I got the house covered. Snow clearin' crews are already out, so you should be able to get back down into the city tomorrow in time to meet me for lunch at the Emerald."

"Excellent," Vertu said cordially. "I will see you then, Cheever." She hesitated. "Thank you for your care," she added.

"You bet," he said after a small pause. "You take care now, hear?"

"I will," she said, and resolutely cut the connection.

The cat was curled tightly in her lap. She sighed, and carefully slipped her hands under its dense, furry body, and moved it carefully to the bench. She then stood, picked up her wine glass and went back to the breakfast room.

Anna and Rascal had joined Mary and Yulie. The hosts were not in sight.

"Left us to ourselfs," said Yulie, "so we don't feel we gotta do the polite. Once Anna's finished eating, we'll just say we're *ready to retire* an' somebody'll come along to show us the way. Got it all set up with Nelirikk for him to take us over to my place tomorrow morning, by snow machine. So, we'll be saying good-night and bye-for-now, Miss Vertu."

"Thank you," she said. "You were wonderful passengers."

"And you were a wonderful driver," Mary said, smiling. "We were fortunate, that it was your cab that we saw, and decided to wait."

"Good-night, Miss Vertu," said Anna, coming to stand at Mary's side, Rascal cuddled in her arms. "Good driving!"

"Thank you for your help," Vertu answered. "Without your Sight, we would have missed the other cab, which would have been very bad."

"Yes," Anna said, and yawned widely.

"I think that's our cue," said Yulie. He bent and picked the fuzzy grey cat from the chair where it was napping. "C'mon, Joey, you're worn right down to bones and claws. Best get to bed."

A shadow moved in the door, murmuring.

"This way, please. We have prepared rooms."

The three of them marched out, and Vertu turned to the buffet to make herself a plate.

She poured another glass of wine, carried it and the plate to a small table, and sat down. She felt something land in her lap, and looked down to see the same multi-colored cat in her lap, looking up in to her face with wide green eyes.

Vertu smiled.

"I suppose you're hungry?" she said.

Scene Three

The Tree Court

It was warm in this place – the Tree Court, according to Jeeves, who had brought them here – and the air smelled of mint and green growing things. There were gloan-roses, just like those at home – on the side of the enclosure opposite the Tree. There was no snow on the short, velvety grass, though the ground was disturbed by humps and hillocks made by the roots closest to the surface.

Toragin hesitated at the edge of the space, basket of cats cuddled against her chest, shivering slightly.

Her anger – her anger on her own behalf – was gone. But for Chelada, and her kittens, she found she could yet be angry.

And so she hesitated, wondering of a sudden if a prudent person would bring anger into this place, or confront the presence that filled this place, like a – well, like a god was said to fill a place holy to her.

She received the idea of gentle laughter, and a sense of soft denial. The Tree was no god, though the Tree had met gods, years and universes gone.

She received the idea that she should come forward, to the Tree's massive trunk, and that she might present her companions.

Careful of her footing among the roots, Toragin did go forward, and knelt in a soft patch of grass at the Tree's base. She settled the basket, and lifted the blanket, glancing up into the leaves.

"This proud mother is Chelada," she said softly. "She gave birth to these four fine kits as we were on the final step of our journey to see your promise to her fulfilled today. They were born in the midst of adventure, but they seem none the worse for it. I have not yet had a chance to do a thorough examination..."

She received the thought that the kittens were beautiful, healthy and free of deformity. After a moment, another such thought inserted itself into her head, that Chelada was likewise beautiful and healthy, and also wise. It put Toragin in mind of one of the elder uncles, who depended upon compliments and charm to rescue him from any social faux pax he might make – and he made many.

"You failed to keep your promise," she said sternly.

What arrived this time was not so much a notion or a thought, but an emotion – dismay, thought Toragin, embarrassment.

Sorrow.

"If you will allow," said Jeeves, the robot who had escorted them to this place. "I am empowered to translate the Tree's – communications – into speech. I offer because the conversation will move more quickly, which you may find desirable, as you are – forgive me – hungry and weary after a very trying day. The Tree would by no means prevent you from enjoying the hospitality of the House, but it wishes to have this matter that lies between it, and yourselves... Balanced as quickly as may be."

"Yes," Toragin said, aware of a grittiness in her eyes, and a certain feeling of ... uncertainty in her thoughts. "Let us by all means come into Balance. Chelada and I had treasured our connection on the homeworld. We had thought we had mattered to the network, that our work was of value. In particular, Chelada had valued the promise that her kittens would be born undertree. To find everything swept aside, without one word, with, so it seemed to me, no thought given to promises made..."

"Precisely," said Jeeves. "The Tree acknowledges its error. It wishes you to know that it is *sorry* – profoundly so – for failing to honor its promises, and also for its failure to properly appreciate work well-done. It would make amends, but it does not know what would be appropriate.

"It asks if you would view some specific action or object as *being* – or perhaps *representing* – amends."

Toragin settled back on her heels, considering the kittens in the basket. She listened for Chelada's voice without very much hope – and thus was surprised.

"Chelada wishes the original promise honored in broad outline," she said slowly. "She would stay, with her kittens – these kittens – undertree and safe until I find a suitable establishment in the city for us. She would also have it that the last-born will remain as her representative to the Tree, to remind it to honor its promises."

There was a small silence before Jeeves spoke.

"The Tree will make these amends and so return to Balance with Chelada."

Toragin inclined her head, realized her eyes were drifting shut and sat up straighter

"And you, Toragin del'Pemridj, what would you have as amends?"

"Consideration for a place in the cat welfare network the Tree has undoubtedly built here, on Surebleak." She squared her shoulders, shook her hair back and stared up into the branches.

"Understand me! I do not want to be given a position – I want fair consideration for a position. Neither I nor Chelada mean to return to Liad. I wish to be of use, which I will never be on Liad. If I cannot be of use to you, I will find something else!"

There was another silence, slightly longer than the first. Jeeves spoke again.

"If you are determined not to return to Liad," he said slowly. "The Tree has a proposition for you…"

ACT NINE

In the Hall of the Mountain King

Vertu drifted slowly toward wakefulness, there being no alarm to insist upon her arising. She smiled, sleepily, and turned her head on the pillow, seeking after the surety of the Tree – just there, on her left, its presence as strong as she had ever felt it.

More, she felt a steady return regard, amused, and oddly tender.

Vertu Dysan, the thought came into her head. *Good morn, neighbor.*

"Good morn," she murmured, and stretched, noting that her left foot was was slightly stiff, which was odd. She would have understood it, had her driving foot been complaining, after yesterday's demands, but this was not her driving foot.

She stretched again – and heard a sneeze from that quadrant.

Carefully, she sat up.

The multi-colored cat was lying half on her foot among the bedclothes. It opened its eyes as if it had felt Vertu's attention, then deliberately squinted them shut.

"I see," she said. "Good morn to you, also, cat. I will be rising in another moment, and dressing, and going to find some tea, and news of the road. It has been pleasant, sharing a bed with you, but all pleasures come to an end."

The cat yawned, showing a wide dainty mouth full of pointed teeth.

Vertu arrived at the breakfast room to find Toragin before her, sipping tea and eating an egg muffin.

"Good morn," she said. "Are the rest of us still abed?"

"Yulie, Mary, Anna, and Rascal left an hour ago, on a snow truck driven by the very large man who is a medic," Toragin said. "Jarome is resting still. The hosts were in, and promise a return after certain of their morning business has been resolved. In the meanwhile, there is news on the comm."

She used her chin to point.

Vertu poured a cup of tea, and approached the comm, being careful of the multi-colored cat, weaving between her feet.

"If you trip me, we will neither escape injury," she said to it.

"She is trying to convince you of her devotion," Toragin said. "She is looking for a quieter place, with a convivial companion, and believes that you will do very well for each other."

Vertu eyed her.

"If you speak cat, please allow – her – to know that my house includes one other individual."

Toragin inclined her head, and murmured. "She does not find that objectionable. I am desired to say that she is a very good hunter, and knows all of the songs for sleeping, and healing, and heart's ease."

"That is an impressive list of accomplishments in one I believe to be quite young. Has she a name, I wonder?"

Toragin smiled slightly.

"She will accept a House name from you."

"Ah," said Vertu, and turned to the news.

"It would appear," she said after some study, "that I may safely return to the city this morning. May I offer you a ride? Or do you and Chelada guest with Korval?"

"Chelada and the kittens guest with the Tree," Toragin said. "I – I have been offered a position, which I am inclined to accept, it being work I enjoy, and which I do well. I will not live here, however, but will need my own establishment, in the city. Might you advise me?"

"I would be honored," said Vertu. "You should know that finding a suitable place may take some time." She hesitated; she remembered the many empty, echoing rooms in her own house.

"If you wish it, you may stay with me while you look for a more pleasing arrangement. I have recently purchased a house, which was once several apartments. There is, right now, myself and occasionally my lover, but that is not enough to keep the house happy."

"That is very generous," said Toragin. "I will accept, and thank you."

"We assist each other," said Vertu. "Neighbor work, as Yulie would have it."

"Yes. I wonder –"

The comm buzzed, and Vertu turned back to it, even as a mellow voice spoke from the vicinity of the ceiling.

"Call for Vertu Dysan, routed to the screen in the breakfast room."

She touched the accept button, and Cheever's face snapped into sharp focus.

"I knew it," he said. "Sleeping in."

"Indeed," she answered with a smile. "Tell me you would do differently."

"Not me. Just callin' to let you know the roads are cleaning up fast. Temps are up and the sun's as bright as can be. You can come on down soon's you're awake."

"I'll do that," she told him, and tipped her head. "Cheever," she said.

"Yeah?"

"I wonder – do you like cats?"

– end –

AUTHORS' COMMENTARY

Stories are strange, wild things, the way we see them, sometimes peeking at us from the distant deep brush and sometimes tracking us down relentlessly, prowling behind our days with the occasional purposeful growl to let us know they are there, waiting, in pursuit of our attention and time. Storytellers know that the story has to be ready to be written, right? They also know that sometimes stories leap out without warning, and must be recounted that way: breathless and sudden.

In the case of "The Gate that Locks the Tree" we'd been hearing the mutterings from the wild for sometime, knowing that yes, sooner or later, we'd need to deal with some of these questions, and some of these characters – after all, had we not seen them drive by in their taxis? Had we not heard them dropping seed pods? Did we not *know*?

And of course, that's what happens with wild things: being wild, they have their own lives. In this case, we knew approximately where the story took place, but not the exact path to get there; we knew some of the habits of the creatures and people involved but not when we might be expected to find them in close proximity, or, in fact, together.

As it happens, the project that became the books *Accepting the Lance* and the still forthcoming *Trader's Leap* provided us with the range of the beast that became "The Gate that Locks the Tree," letting us know the season it would be most evident to us, and giving us the penetrating vision to see that it was time we shook these elements together: a Liaden's first look at snow, a Tree's memory of promises to a distant pet, the matter of necessity when it came to dealing with things set in motion years before, and of course, Surebleak's tendency to bend burgeoning event to unanticipated outcome.

Let it be known that in this wild hunt when the first word was typed we knew only that Vertu, the Tree, and a promise were involved. Of a morning Vertu's extensive Liaden backstory reminded us that while to most of Surebleak the Tree was a new and unusual thing, to Vertu it was something more – to her it was the commonplace oddity of her youth, a comfort as she'd driven on Liad and now, there again in her sky, a landmark.

And knowing the Tree was Vertu's landmark meant it had to be such for other folk, too, and suddenly the wild hunt became something we had to write now (despite novels in progress at the time!) and the story tumbled out of the bush, with characters old and new, with storyteller insight that *we* needed to know this stuff so other things could happen, elsewhere and elsewhen.

This story comes to you then as an example of the "And there we were!" of a personal experience, as delivered over a glass, comfortably distant now that it's done. Consider it a telling of what happened on a cold and snowy day on Surebleak, to people with connections to a universe that's both far away and immediate.

We hope you've enjoyed the story.

STEVE MILLER AND SHARON LEE
Cat Farm and Confusion Factory
February 2020

ABOUT THE AUTHORS

Maine-based writers Sharon Lee and Steve Miller teamed up in the late 1980s to bring the world the story of Kinzel, an inept wizard with a love of cats, a thirst for justice, and a staff of true power.

Since then, the husband-and-wife team have written dozens of short stories and twenty plus novels, most set in their star-spanning, nationally-bestselling, Liaden Universe®.

Before settling down to the serene and stable life of a science fiction and fantasy writer, Steve was a traveling poet, a rock-band reviewer, reporter, and editor of a string of community newspapers.

Sharon, less adventurous, has been an advertising copywriter, copy editor on night-side news at a small city newspaper, reporter, photographer, and book reviewer.

Both credit their newspaper experiences with teaching them the finer points of collaboration.

Steve and Sharon are jointly the recipients of the E. E. "Doc" Smith Memorial Award for Imaginative Fiction (the Skylark), one of the oldest awards in science fiction. In addition, their work has won the much-coveted Prism Award (*Mouse and Dragon* and *Local Custom*), as well as the Hal Clement Award for Best Young Adult Science Fiction (*Balance of Trade*), and the Year's Best Military and Adventure SF Readers' Choice Award ("Wise Child").

Sharon and Steve passionately believe that reading fiction ought to be fun, and that stories are entertainment.

Steve and Sharon maintain a web presence at: http://korval.com

NOVELS BY SHARON LEE AND STEVE MILLER

The Liaden Universe®

Fledgling
Saltation
Mouse and Dragon
Ghost Ship
Dragon Ship
Necessity's Child
Trade Secret
Dragon in Exile
Alliance of Equals
The Gathering Edge
Neogenesis
Accepting the Lance
Trader's Leap

Omnibus Editions

The Dragon Variation
The Agent Gambit
Korval's Game
The Crystal Variation

Story Collections

A Liaden Universe Constellation: Volume 1
A Liaden Universe Constellation: Volume 2
A Liaden Universe Constellation: Volume 3
A Liaden Universe Constellation: Volume 4

The Fey Duology

Duainfey
Longeye

Gem ser'Edreth

The Tomorrow Log

NOVELS BY SHARON LEE

The Carousel Trilogy

Carousel Tides
Carousel Sun
Carousel Seas

Jennifer Pierce Maine Mysteries

Barnburner
Gunshy

THANK YOU

Thank you for your support of our work.

Sharon Lee and Steve Miller

Made in the USA
Middletown, DE
27 December 2020

30233385R00061